Santa Claus: The King of the Elves

Abridged Children's Edition

BY

B.C.CHASE

B.C.CHASE is the internationally bestselling author of the *Paradeisia Trilogy* which critics have hailed as one of the greatest franchises of our time.* His electrifying talent for combining the latest in scientific breakthroughs with edge-of-your-seat thrills has earned him a reputation as a master of suspense. Amazon has ranked him #1 in Religion and Spirituality, among its top ten Sci-fi authors, and a top 20 writer of Thrillers.

"B.C.CHASE IS RAPIDLY BECOMING AN AUTHOR OF AUTHORITY."
GRADY HARP, VINE VOICE

"CHASE HAS MASTERED THE ART OF WRITING SUSPENSE."
L.A. HOWELL

"IN TRUE CRICHTON STYLE, CHASE TAKES ELEMENTS OF KNOWN SCIENCE, EXPLORES THEIR EXTREME POTENTIAL, AND BUILDS A MYSTERY AROUND SCIENTIFIC PRINCIPLES."
-AMAZON.COM

"CHASE HAS TALENT YOU WON'T SOON FORGET."
-AMAZON.COM

"CHASE IS A BRILLIANT WRITER WITH A BOATLOAD OF TALENT."
-VINCENT VERITAS

"CHASE KEEPS YOU WANTING MORE."
-DEBRA HANSEN

Also by B.C.CHASE:

Leviathan
Glass
Paradeisia: Origin of Paradise
Paradeisia: Violation of Paradise
Paradeisia: Fall of Paradise
Catatan
Santa Claus: The King of the Elves (Unabridged)

*Epub.us

Preseption Press

ISBN: 1548073814

This is a work of fiction. Corporations, characters, organizations, or other entities in this novel are the product of the author's imagination, or, if real, are used fictitiously without any intent to describe their actual conduct.

For Blake

Contents

Pronunciation Guide

(Some of these characters, creatures, and places are found only in the unabridged edition of this book.)

Names

Beliach: BEHL-ee-awkh
Bompus: BAWM-puhs
Bufus: BUE-fuhs
Dantor: DAN-tor
Dryrie: DRY-ree
Faybin: FAY-bin
Garbella: gahr-BELL-uh
Grimunwald: GRIMM-uhn-wahld
Grygor: GRAHY-gohr
Jaylit: JAY-lit
Karbondor: KAHR-buhn-door
Kelia: KEL-ee-uh
Kintel: KIN-tell
Linnea: LYNN-ey-uh
Lannolith: LAWN-oh-lith
Myckel: MICK-ell
Prelanopy: Pree-LAN-oh-pee
Roatark: ROE-tarck
Ruthorspat: RUH-thawr-spat
Thrushti: THRUSH-tee
Viardech: Vee-ARH-dekh

Creatures

Bumbodorf: BUHM-boh-dorf
Psylodont: SIGH-loh-dawnt
Murleith: MUR-lythe
Tawdle: TAW-dl
Screekaw: SCREE-caw
Ushvark: UHSH-vark

Places:

Ashet: ASH-eht
Bannonith: BAN-oh-nith
Balekhon: BAHL-ay-khawn
Duzenfald: DOO-zen-fawld
Euchaia: YOO-kay-uh
Kizdel: KIZ-del
Leytholin: LEY-thoh-lin
Lyadeth: LIE-uh-deth
Malach: Mawl-AWKH
Meteran: MET-er-an
Sevant: SAY-vant
Simindra: Sim-IN-druh
Ufratin: yoo-FREYT-in

Preface

There have been many stories about the life of Santa Claus, but none of them is entirely true and most of them are fancifully false. The remarkable reality of this wondrous character is not what you might expect: it is a perilous adventure full of the kinds of frightful and extraordinary things one reads about in farfetched novels authored by dusty old professors with extremely vivid imaginations. The difference here is that this is not fantasy. Through an extensive, quite dangerous and very expensive venture I have catalogued all the details. Thus it is in the following pages that I am able to present, quite faithfully, an accurate narrative of the birth and marvelous triumph of that indomitable spirit who has, through the ages, been the bearer of gifts and magic for young and old and who will always be the greatest champion of that most miraculous of holidays that happily never fails to fall on the 25th of December. Some of the writing here, I must confess, is not my own, but is derived from ancient manuscripts that my travels uncovered.

Before I continue, however, I must provide a clear warning: the true story of Santa Claus is perilous, indeed. There are no frolicking reindeer, no jingling elves, no tidy ribbons or bows.... Santa was a hero and as such his tale is epic. So if you want to avoid being frightened nearly out of your wits, then do not proceed. But if it is your wish, I respectfully give you the true story of Santa Claus.

-B.C.

SANTA CLAUS: THE KING OF THE ELVES

ALSO DON'T MISS THE UNABRIDGED EDITION TO THE #1 BESTSELLING CHRISTMAS BOOK ON AMAZON.COM

When Santa's true love, Linnea, is kidnapped, he and his loyal High Elf friends embark on an enthralling journey across the perilous lands of Euchaia in a desperate bid to bring her safely home. But they do not realize that much more is at stake than Linnea's life. By the end, the very survival of all

High Elves is in jeopardy and Santa must make a fateful choice between his love for Linnea and the destiny of the elves.

In this spellbinding adventure, internationally bestselling author B.C.CHASE taps the furthest reaches of his mesmerizing imagination to weave a suspenseful tale featuring seafaring dwarves, fiery dragons, cultured goblins, and flying elves that culminates in a battle of epic proportions.

Prologue

Long, long ago beyond the realms of memory in ages lost to time, a great elf of renown lived in the tranquil cedar forests of the west. Myckel was his name, and he was one of the few elves who retained knowledge of how to read the prophesies written in the stars. From a lofty perch among the highest branches of a mighty and gently swaying tree, he beheld a wondrous sign in the stars—what he knew in the wisdom of his long life to be a revelation foretelling what only the stars and their maker could tell.

The Morning Star lifted from the beautiful, blue Euchaia and the White Captives arose.

Upon seeing this, Myckel left the beautiful forest of the west to take up watch in the far northern wilderlands where cold winds and icy blizzards made habitation difficult for everyone (notwithstanding the snowy owls and arctic foxes).

When Myckel arrived, not one human and very few elves lived there. But as the centuries passed, the summers grew warmer and the glaciers began to melt, releasing great rivers of roaring water that irrigated the plains and valleys below and caused lush green grass to grow and radiant flowers to blossom where once had been stone, frost, and lichen.

An adventurer wandering into these freshly fertile

wilderlands discovered flakes of pure gold in the rivers, and the rumor of his discovery spread furiously through the ranks of men who, until that time had relied solely upon the dwarves for the coveted treasure. There soon swelled a great migration of men. Carried by horses, mules, and their own callused feet they came, drove after drove of hopeful souls with few resources and even fewer skills. Despite their shortcomings, because of the easy accessibility of the gold, they were quite prosperous, for a time. Dark Elven traders from the south furnished them with a relentless supply of the finest foods, wines, and exotic luxuries that gold could buy. They were extraordinarily rich.

But the enduring paradox of wealth is that the more one accumulates, the more one worries about its preservation, so the people began to fear the worst in all its forms: plagues, droughts, floods, and the like. Cultic priests arose from among them and introduced the worship of deities of prosperity and power and indulgence. They erected giant stones on the top of a great hill and built an altar at a place they called Bannonith.

They were not wise with their riches. Trade was frenetic and frivolous and no foundation was laid for the future. Thus, in the course of time, their worst fears were realized when the glaciers stopped melting and the supply of gold flakes was exhausted. The immigrants faced a very sudden and very overwhelming destitution. With gold scarce and food swiftly growing scarcer, they became desperate in their worship of the gods. The priests advised more and more sacrifices to appease them, so the people sacrificed everything in sight, even those things which might have been their deliverance: their crops, their animals, and even, I am very distressed to report, their own children.

The elven traders who had before supplied the wilderland settlers with more than they could possibly consume now demanded payment for the substantial debts the settlers had accumulated. Finding the immigrants impoverished, the traders raided the villages in the dark of night and took everything they could, stopping at nothing in their quest for retribution.

But this was not the end of trouble. For generations, the settlers survived as well as they could by planting small, short-lived summer gardens, by hunting, and by foraging. The gods were forgotten and the sacrifices ceased, but the Dark Elven traders formed marauding gangs armed with the quickest and surest of arrows, the sharpest of swords, and the cruelest of contempt for human life. With regular frequency, they stormed the villages in search of their quarry, malicious and merciless. The Dark Elves left the people with nothing more than the looming fear of their return.

Thus, the people of the wilderlands became cold and hardened, with wearied eyes always watching to the south for black horses and dark riders, and the births of babies met with dread rather than with joy.

Chapter One

One still night, Myckel and his loyal friend Kintel, whose bright eyes were always full of empathy and care, and whose loyalty and courage had never been in question, were sneaking through the forest looking for the best patches of starlight in which to restore their ever-waning energy.

Suddenly streaking across the sky was a bright light that cast foreboding, scraggly tree shadows on the snowy white ground. It was a shooting star, with a long tail of white flame billowing behind it. The star appeared to fall near Bannonith, so, with curiosity as their companion, the two elves made for the hill, though it was a great distance away.

Upon reaching the towering assembly of giant stones, now a forgotten vestige of the old superstitions, overgrown and decayed from disuse, through the lightly falling flakes of snow, a sound to which Myckel was not accustomed reached his elven ears. It was the distinctive little cry of a newborn babe, helpless and pitiable. As they drew near it, they saw upon the cold stone altar a child, its bare skin exposed to the icy air and its breaths rising into the blackness as small, frantic puffs of vapor.

Myckel's fearsome gray eyes gazed fatefully at the

infant. The kicks of its tiny legs and the thrashes of its tiny arms waned with every moment. The bitter cold would soon claim its young life.

Having little regard for the human race and little concern for their affairs and troubles, Myckel turned away with the intention never to look back. But then, after the furrow of a brow and a pensive moment of thought, he returned his countenance. He walked to the altar and gazed down upon the infant. Its eyes were scarcely open, so recent was its birth.

But there was something extraordinary about this human babe—something almost terrifying in its implications, something that had been foretold in the prophesies of the ancient past.

Having never held a babe (since elves do not have children), he clumsily lifted the child from the chilly stone and wrapped it under his cloak.

Now, the elves were a cursed race. You see, they were meant to fly. The earth was not their home at all, but in ancient times they used to travel the universe in all its glory and see the wonders of heaven. In the beginning they were free to travel anywhere they wished, to see any sight they desired, to sip the nectar of any world, to bathe in the water of any planet and, best of all, to listen to the singing of the stars and live in the light of their maker, the Morning Star. But there was one place that was forbidden to them, one world they were not to touch. That was Euchaia.

It was said that if they chose to step foot on this world, they would be imprisoned, never able to leave. Euchaia was not made for them and, therefore, was not theirs to claim.

The name of the elf who first lighted on Euchaia and lost their freedom was Beliach. Before he fell, he had been the greatest, wisest and most beautiful of the elves. Afterwards, he had enacted a deceitful campaign to convince the elves that there was no curse and that they were *meant* to be on Euchaia. There were many elves who were deceived by him and who became his agents of wickedness deceiving others. Beliach was successful also in his deception because only one elf had been there to see him as he first lighted on Euchaia, and she was much smaller and weaker than he.

Her name was Kelia. After Beliach had destroyed her, the beauty of her wings and sweetness of her spirit were nearly forgotten by all but two, Beliach himself and Myckel, who had been her dearest friend—and neither ever spoke of her, the former out of pride and the latter out of pain. Whether it be for the sake of curiosity, or envy, or the simple delight in doing something which is forbidden, or, most pitiably, in order to try to rescue those who had already fallen, one by one each and every elf landed on Euchaia, and each and every elf lost his freedom. Black circles appeared around their wrists, shackles that kept them bound to Euchaia no matter how hard they tried to fly. The wings of the elves began to tighten and shred with disuse until they had totally fallen away from all but a few. Those who still had wings could hardly boast that they were wings at all because of their despicable condition. In fact, any elf with wings left who did not sneak away to secretly tear away the remnants of his wings was doomed to a life of sorrowful mockery or solitude or, at the hand of Beliach's Dark Elves, even death.

Because Beliach was cleverer and greater than any of the other elves, the first of his kind, he had seen a prophesy of the Morning Star, a rescuer that would come to destroy him and free the elves from their bondage on Euchaia. For this reason, in addition to purging the elven world of the memory of his treachery, his agents were always listening for any warning of the appearance of this Morning Star. Beliach lived in Balekhon with his legions of Dark Elves always waiting, always watching so that, either by fear or by death, none should enter the interminable pit there known as the Deep of Balekhon, for this was the place where was foretold Beliach's fate and destruction would be sealed.

As Myckel and Kintel made their swift flight through the forest, they worried that the babe seemed increasingly pale.

"What shall we do?" Kintel asked his friend as they hastily made their way through the dark woods.

"I know someone who can care for it."

"What's wrong with it?" Kintel asked. "It isn't moving much." This was indeed true for the tiny face was now deathly pale and the arms and legs almost limp.

"It needs nourishment," said Myckel. "And warmth."

"What does it eat?"

Myckel paused. He frowned, "Something we don't have."

"Would nuts or berries do?" Kintel suggested hopefully. His greatest loathing was to see others suffer.

"No."

"He looks frightfully ill," noted Kintel, appearing that he might burst into tears.

"We must hurry. Time is closing in."

With ever increasing urgency, they raced through the dark woods and, at length, reached an abode on the edge of a town. It had a colorful array of stained glass windows and a steep roof of pine shingles. The sun was making its first appearance in the eastern horizon as Myckel knocked on the door.

It was answered by a diminutive person with a large head and an even larger hat. He had big, flappy ears like the ears of elephants which, at the sight of Myckel, popped out in alarm and quivered—like two banners in a fierce breeze. His face, which was round with kindly, bulging eyes and a wrinkly nose with nostrils wide apart, paled dramatically.

Tawdles (for that is what he was) were little people who, though not significant in number, were an essential part of the societies of men, elves, and dwarves. They were masters of medicine, devoting most of their time to the collection and study of all manner of herbs, fungi, venoms, saps, minerals, and flowers. They had, over the years, developed a deep knowledge of healing, and were relied upon by the sick and injured for tonics and brews to alleviate and sometimes even cure ailments of all kinds. Because of their intrinsic value as such, they had no enemies among the other peoples and were able to live peaceably and prosperously no matter where they settled. They were highly opinionated, but congenial; a bit parsimonious, but indulgent, and in possession of a peculiar yet fascinating fondness for hats of all shapes and sizes. They were also skilled glassblowers and crafted wonderful stained ornaments and objects of all kinds.

Myckel, without bothering to engage in formal niceties, said, "You know me, Mr. Claus, do you not?"

The startled tawdle stuttered, "I—no I do not. Never set eyes on you in my life."

Mr. Claus tried to close the door, but Myckel braced his arm upon it, saying, "Indeed you do, for it was I who rescued you from the tree that was about to fall upon you. You are indebted to me." He pushed past befuddled and perplexed Mr. Claus and strode into the room, which was warmly illuminated by beautiful stained glass lamps and sconces. Over little burners and on stoves were a vast assortment of glass bottles, decanters, and chalices bubbling and steaming with translucent liquids. The tawdle's wife, wearing a fluffy hat, looked down on them from a loft with a banister of iron and colorful glass.

Myckel lay the babe on a wooden table and stood back, folding his arms. "I found this child on the altar at Bannonith."

"Bannonith?" the anxious tawdle exclaimed, dread filling his voice. "On the *altar*?"

The child, looking quite helpless, cried and flailed its little arms and legs about like an overturned beetle. The tawdle's wife rushed down a flight of crudely manufactured wooden steps spiraling down a tree trunk. She cried, "You can't drop a baby on a table like a stuck pig!" She swooped the child up in her arms and soothed, "There, there."

Myckel said to the man, "You owe me a life-debt." He nodded to the babe, "Keep this child. Raise him as your own. When he is ready, I will return for him. A life for a life."

"But we have our own little mouths to feed," the tawdle protested, lowering his ears to the sides of his face like a shawl and holding his hat in his hands in front of his chest. "Times are hard. Food is scarce."

"Food is so scarce, and yet your children are so well-fed," Myckel replied, looking up at a row of three chubby tawdles wearing soft nighttime linens and hats, now peering down from the balustrade.

"But this child is no tawdle! How are we to care for him?"

"He is not safe in the company of men. He must stay hidden."

"But the Dark Elf raiders—" Mr. Claus said anxiously, "They are always on the prowl for the children of men. I don't want them prowling around here! What of them?"

"I will protect you."

"But—"

"But what?" the tawdle's wife interrupted. She was feeding the child from a glass bottle with a linen nozzle. "He needs our help! Are you so hard-hearted you would turn away a poor, helpless babe?"

The tawdle, looking quite flummoxed, shrugged and said, "A life for a life. But don't forget to come get him when he's older!"

Myckel did not specify the date of his return nor his plans for the grown boy, but he warned the Clauses that the baby was a child of destiny and should be kept secret as long as possible.

As they left, Kintel asked, "Are you sure he is the one?"

Myckel replied, "The prophesy foretells of a child both elven and human. His eyes are blue and certainly human, but he has elven ears. He is half-human, half-elven."

Almost as if Myckel had said something shameful, Kintel exclaimed, "But that's impossible!"

"And yet the prophesies foretell it. This is the child. There is no doubt."

Chapter Two

Under the care of Mr. and Mrs. Claus the babe was the contented recipient of much doting and affection. Mr. Claus was unable to resist its coos and smiles, despite himself. They named him Santa (a fitting addition to their own children Banta, Lanta, and Kanta) and, without reservation, considered him their own.

Unfortunately, what might have been a relatively unencumbered childhood became less so due to the danger of his being discovered, for rumor of his birth reached Beliach, who dispatched his darkest agents with the dreadful mission to find and slay every single infant boy from the north to the south. Fortunately, the tawdles were never suspected. Among men, however, the slaughter was great, indeed. Thus, the New Year was brought in not with celebration and hope, but with cries of agony in every home from cabins to castles. From that time on, the elves were hated by men with a deep and terrible rage.

Since the time of Santa's birth, events conspired to make life treacherous for the Good Elves, for not only was their health deteriorating with the lack of starlight, but their very existence was threatened.

Beliach's brutal murder of all the young boys had

left a deep scar on humanity's impression of the elves, for men did not distinguish between the Good Elves and the Dark Elves, but looked upon them all with the same malice. Thus, a campaign of annihilation was launched against them. The Good Elves, as a result, kept themselves so secret that men quickly altered course from seeking their elimination to congratulating themselves on having eliminated them. The Dark Elves, on the other hand, did what was necessary to assimilate into human society, engaging in black market trade and supplying slave labor to those with the money to pay—especially in the wealthy kingdom of Balekhon.

In the wilderlands, the boy Claus steadily grew into a cheerful, hearty young man. With time, his Tawdle parents lowered their guard and allowed Santa to mingle with his own kind. Mrs. Claus toiled away for hours over a white cap that he could wear to keep his ears warm because, in addition to their unusually long and pointy appearance as compared to the human children with which he sometimes insisted upon fraternizing with notwithstanding his parent's protests, they had a tendency of freezing dreadfully. On his first mammoth hunt (a rite of passage for the human boys of those parts), Santa faced no small harassment when, grappling with one of the giant beasts at the end of a spear, his cap fell off his head and his ears were exposed in all their elven glory. His fellow hunters mocked his ears, but no matter how cruel it became, he did not open his mouth. In fact, nobody ever said that he heard an unkind or selfish word from Santa.

The Clauses' tawdle children loved the boy Santa dearly. Since he grew quicker and taller than they, they frequently called upon him to carry them or to toss them in the air, their big tawdle ears flapping in the breeze as they giggled in delight. His own merry laugh, which is now famous the world over, came to be a hallmark of his persona.

Despite his tawdle father's efforts to train him in glassmaking, Santa was much more skilled with wood and was always eager to help anyone with the crafting of a new set of furniture or a beautiful mantelpiece. He always carried an axe with him when he was out of doors just so that if he spotted a superior piece of lumber he could chop it down and drag it home with the help of reindeer who, oddly, seemed to be at his service whenever he called for them.

While his skill with the axe and chisel were great indeed, perhaps his preeminent asset was his ability to tell stories. Often, after a long day of hard labor out in the sunny cold, all the families in the vicinity would gather in one home and, when everyone had hung their stockings up to dry from the wet snow, Santa would set a stool down sturdy at the hearth, take a child or two on his lap and tell stories that were wondrous and wise. Some of his stories concerned elves, quite a frightening prospect for his listeners since they were such a taboo topic among men.

The most peculiar aspect of Santa's character was that several times a year he would venture into the woods and disappear, not returning for days or even weeks. What he did there has never been fully explained nor understood, but the wise say that he would gaze at the stars and see wondrous things in them and that he would hear voices from far away calling across space and time. Perhaps he never fully felt whole with men. He seemed, in some way, incomplete.

And now would be a very good time to share with you a most important part of the story of Santa Claus. Linnea was her name, and how he came to know her was no small adventure in and of itself.

She had been born in a small village in the wilderlands and was, in most respects, a victim of her parents' mindless, endless search for riches. In her childhood, she had not known love because the only thing her parents loved was gold. Their obsession had become so complete that she went without a word from them for days while they worried and wondered about where next to search or what next to sift. She had no time for play as some children do, but instead spent every moment trying to cultivate roots and tubers for eating. One day, rumor of Dark Elves seen on the horizon spread like wildfire among the village, and her parents fled the house to secure their golden hordes. That night, they did not return.

After many tumultuous days of insecurity and neglect, little Linnea made her way shivering and starving through frigid winds to the south in search of a distant aunt. Unfortunately, her aunt had also fallen victim to the Dark Elven raid. It seemed she had lost so much that even her mind's whereabouts were unknown. Her madness was, in one respect, a positive improvement on her, up to that time severe, character in that she had become incessantly happy and optimistic. It is a well-known fact that someone mad but glad is far better company than someone sane but sad, so she made for a cheery companion—though she could not be relied upon to tend the garden or do anything industrious except weaving and knitting, both of which she did very poorly.

Her aunt's abode was but a hollow in the ground with stones and sticks piled up around and atop it. There was no window because there was no glass, and the crude door hung loosely with breezy cracks all around. Inside were two beds of straw, a pit for a fire, a simple table, and a bench for sitting on. A copper pot, some wooden cups and spoons, and a cracked knife were stored in a basket by the door. Curiously, on the table was a silver goblet and plate which she always kept in the same place, never used and never washed. When Linnea had arrived, there had been an elegant rocking chair and some other furniture, but Linnea had traded these for a sheep. When she tried to sell the silver goblet and the silver plate, her aunt went into such a fit of hysterics that she quickly relented, fearing her poor aunt would pull every last hair out of her head.

Linnea had applied a great deal of time and effort to transforming a patch of weeds by the house into a garden. Whenever she entered the door, her aunt would say, "Any gold today, my dear?" to which Linnea, having learned through trial and error to avoid explaining that she was gardening and not gold-sifting, simply said, "No, not yet."

Her aunt, always the optimist, never failed to reply, "Don't worry, my dear. It will turn up!"

Through the course of these arduous years, Linnea had blossomed from young lass to graceful lady. Tending gardens and milking sheep and scouring pots and beating clothes and carrying water buckets was not very graceful work, but Linnea herself, no matter what she did, had such grace about her that, once he made her acquaintance, Santa was entirely entranced. She was passionate in everything and there was no emotion which she did not express in the most emphatic of terms. There was nothing about which she did not have an immediate opinion and from one moment to the next she could change her role or attitude. She either absolutely hated something or she absolutely loved it, she either jumped and danced for joy or wept and wailed for sorrow, she was either repentant beyond reason or would never apologize ever, she was either nigh unto death with illness or positively bursting with health, she was either sharper than the sharpest tack or . . . well, in short, she was a marvel and it was not long after he met her that Santa came to be a willing servant to any wish she expressed. Linnea, though polite, showed no affection in response to his attention, but rather assigned him tasks, such as hoeing the garden or delivering buckets of fresh water from the spring a long walk away.

Among his first concerns was to assemble a new rocking chair for her aunt. After this followed more furniture until, at length, the hut was quite suitably well-appointed.

One day, Linnea was doing her best to milk the

sheep. I say "doing her best" because, as anyone who has tried to milk a sheep before can tell you, sheep's milk is a valuable prize due not only to its mild and wholesome taste, but also because of the naturally skittish nature of its manufacturers.

On this day, matters were worse than usual. The sheep's eyes were open wide, darting hither and thither in a constant search for danger, and its legs were kicking here and there as if ready to leap into action at the slightest sound. Linnea had been unable to coax even a single drop of milk from it when the sheep suddenly bolted, tearing away up the hillside as if a pack of ferocious wolves was in hot pursuit.

She jumped up and, with a sigh, gathered her skirt to chase after it, but stopped when she had a very odd and disconcerting feeling that she was being watched. And indeed she was, for on the rise behind her was a gang of Dark Elvish raiders, hooded and tall and daunting astride their stamping black horses. One of the horses neighed—a terrible, shrieking sound, and launched its sprint down the hill, the dark figure atop it armed with a silvery, curved sabre that glinted in the light of the sun. In his other hand, the elf held a shackle for her neck.

You see, the elven raids were of the vilest sort, for they came not in search of property or goods, but in search of human life. They took as many of the youngest and the fairest as they could, all to be sold as laborers in the kingdom of Balekhon to the distant south. The hostages were dragged away with their hands tied behind their backs and their necks chained together like oxen, never to be seen nor heard from again.

Santa was in the woods that day, as he usually was, and heard Linnea's voice as clearly as if she was right next to him. With desperation and terror, she was screaming his name. Elves, you see, have excellent hearing, magical hearing, if you will, so much so that when anyone calls to an elf, no matter how great the distance, the sound always reaches the ears of the one called. Santa, therefore, could hear her cry, but he knew not whence it came. He would have called back to her, but of course she would not have heard him because she was no elf. Without delay, he mounted a reindeer and rode with furious haste for her abode.

When he arrived, he was greeted by her aunt at the gate who, in the greatest of distress cried out, "They took her! The Dark Elves! *They took her!*"

"Which way did they go?" Santa demanded from atop his steed.

The hapless aunt, blubbering and whimpering, looked to the ground.

“Which way?” Santa shouted, his reindeer anxiously stamping beneath him.

“I do not know!” the poor woman cried, cupping her face in her hands. “I cannot remember!”

Santa leaped to the ground beside her and, placing his hand on her back, compassionately said, “Come, come into the house.”

He led her inside and sat her on her rocking chair. “Please, you must try to remember,” he implored, gazing into her face.

“I cannot!” she wailed. Her hand shook as she put it to her forehead.

Santa fetched a cup of water from the bucket and offered it to her, “Here, drink this. Do not fret.”

The aunt obliged, sipping the drink and taking a breath.

Santa stared at her expectantly.

Hopping off her chair, she exclaimed, “I have seen it!” and rushed outside. She pointed in the direction of the hill, “That way!”

“Bannonith,” Santa said in a low voice. He leapt astride his reindeer, who seemed to know which way to go without being told and galloped up the hill with tremendous speed. The aunt, after watching him depart, hands wringing together under her chin, went into the house and stared down at the cup and bowl that sat, as they always did, on the table. “I lost you so long ago!" she said, tears streaming down her cheeks. "I cannot lose Linnea this way! It is too much to bear!" And with that, she fell on her knees, overcome by weeping.

With her hands pinioned behind her, Linnea was pulled up an ancient stone path leading to the imposing, erect stones of Bannonith. Around her neck was a shackle linked to a heavy chain that was fastened to the saddle of the black horse. The horse's tail flicked in her face as she struggled to keep pace with it. She never caught a glimpse of the elf's face who sat astride it, though she heard his fearsome voice as he hissed at her, "Keep up!" and saw the glint of his black eyes from under his hood. The other Dark Elves addressed him as "Viardech."

Once they were inside the perimeter of giant stones, all the people the Dark Elves had collected, male and female, were joined together by their chains. None of them dared attempt an escape due to the glinting sabers the elves clanged on the chains, sending showers of sparks in all directions, and the poison-infused arrows they carried, said to magically reach whomever they were fired upon no matter how poorly the elves aimed them.

Linnea, however, already having lost her parents

to the elven raids, knew the likely fate of those who were brought to Balekhon. She struggled against her bonds with increasing panic, tearfully beseeching their dark captors to spare them. The leader, Viardech, wearying of her cries, dismounted from his horse. He shouted, "Silence!" and he struck her. His long, black nails left three red streaks across her cheek and she was thrown to the limit of her chains, the shackle cutting into her neck. The Dark Elf raised his hand for another blow, but from the base of the hill a voice loud and defiant bellowed, "Let her alone!"

The Dark Elf's hood turned as he cast his gaze towards the voice. Standing there was a man with a white hat on his head, wearing no armor, and holding nothing in his hands but an axe. A large and powerful, breathlessly panting reindeer stood beside him.

The elf laughed and took several steps around the prisoners towards the man, "Who are you?"

The man slipped the white cap off his head, revealing his elven ears. "Let them go," he said.

From the blackness under his hood, the elf's eyes could be seen glinting with wicked zeal, "Let them go? And why should we do that?" His elven kin joined him to stand between the monumental stones that towered high above them.

"Let the people go!" the man repeated,

The Viardech looked at his companions and

started to laugh.

Linnea blinked tears down her cheeks, her eyes hopeless. "Santa," she cried, "they will kill you!"

Viardech nocked an arrow, raised his bow, and released the string. The arrow whizzed through the air directly towards Santa, but he easily deflected it with his axe. Viardech nodded to two of his companions who fired their arrows upon Santa in unison. The arrows sailed towards him, but as they reached him they veered to the sides, crossed behind him, and flew back around to pierce the hearts of those who had fired them. They fell to the ground.

"You use black magic to power your arrows," said Santa, "but your dark deeds will always find you out. He who lives by the sword will die by the sword."

"Who are you?" Viardech demanded, his voice spewing from inside his black cloak like a spiteful sneer.

Santa clenched his fist around his axe, his jaw set with determination, and his eyes blazing like white hot flames. A booming crack suddenly sounded as a fracture split across the stone face like a bolt of lightning. The top half of the stone slid off to collide with the stone beside it, which also cracked. In this way each stone was split into halves which collided with their neighbors until the last stone ruptured, its top half grinding off directly above the group of elves, who scampered forward to avoid being crushed. As the giant stone landed behind them with a thunderous boom, they beheld Santa with a great deal more respect than they had previously.

"Get on your horses," Santa said, his eyes now no longer blazing nor white, but certainly still furious, "and leave the wilderlands."

With a glance of defiance at Santa, the Viardech nodded to his companions. Then they wasted not a moment as they rushed to leap atop their stallions. They raced into the distance, and Santa ran into the center of the stones to free the prisoners.

No sooner had he released the bonds from Linnea's wrists then, with her neck still shackled, she spun around and threw her arms around his neck, crying into his chest. It was on that day, I think, that she truly began to trust that he loved her, and to love him in return.

So it was that the families gathered to celebrate the safe return of the captives. To Santa was given a large white coat with fur trim that had been carefully crafted by his mother to match the white cap she had made for him all those years ago. A large, blazing bonfire was built and the choicest of mammoth meat was roasted. Each and every person had his fill and then, with every ear pricked and every face eager, Santa related his most cherished story of all. They heard his voice and saw the twinkle in his eye as he told of angels and shepherds and wise men and a soon-to-be mother and father with nowhere to stay and a newborn child in a feeding trough that would grow up to be the good shepherd who would lay his life down for his sheep. But in this, of course, he was merely making a prophesy.

When he finished this story, everyone was preparing to go back to his own home for the night. He took Linnea aside, wrapped her up warmly, and led her out the door. With her hand in his, he strode under the starlit sky and through the woods to a grassy glade overlooking a tree-lined valley. There, situated perfectly in the moonlight, was a new cabin made of the finest cedar logs and cedar shingles. He spoke in great detail of the intricacies of every labor and every thought he had devoted to its construction. He did not specifically state that it was built with Linnea in mind, but his frequent, hopeful pauses for approving words or gestures (which Linnea was careful not to reward) indicated as much. When he finished, he stepped back and surveyed his work and the woman beside it, and, with a nod, folded his arms. But not a word came from Linnea, so he cleared his throat and shuffled his feet a bit. When still no word came, he said simply, “What say you?”

But she said nothing because tears were

streaming down her cheeks, so happy and so grateful was she.

Meanwhile, back at the Clauses' home, a tap was heard on the Claus's door. As was customary during the late evening, Mr. Claus, his large tawdle ears wide open, was the one to answer it. There, with a pale face shining ghostly in the moonlight and two gray eyes peering out from under a hood was Myckel. He quietly said, "The time has come. I am here for the boy."

Chapter Three

Mr. Claus quickly came to the door and, with first a gasp, and then one disgruntled glance from his face to his feet and back to his face again, said, "What do you mean coming here in the middle of the night like this?"

Myckel stepped forward into the room and, despite their displeasure, the Clauses were forced to make way. He said, "When I brought the babe I told you that he was a child of destiny and that I would return. The time has come."

Mrs. Claus was flabbergasted, "The time for what? Foolish elf magic and wizardry?"

"The time has come for him to *choose*," Myckel said. "He alone can claim his destiny."

Mrs. Claus, face reddened and ears fully unfurled, rushed up and said, "Well I don't know what destiny you've concocted for him but he's quite happy where he is, thank you very much. In fact, he's been taking a liking to a very sweet girl from nearby if that tells you anything."

Myckel raised a brow, "What does his father say?"

Mr. Claus said softly, "Santa is of age. Let him speak for himself."

"Where is he?"

"Oh, out with the reindeer, I suppose. We have

ne'er been able to keep him inside a'night since he could walk."

"I will wait," Myckel said, and stood against a wall with his long arms crossed and his gray eyes closed.

When it became apparent that Myckel would not be budged from his position (despite the many cries of protest and budges that Mrs. Claus produced), she was left with no alternative but to wait for Santa to arrive.

And arrive he did, an hour or so later. Mrs. Claus's pleadings, scoldings, and guilt heaps were not enough to stop Santa from following the elf out into the dark of the night for a furtive dialogue.

"Speak, elf," said Santa, "and I will listen."

Myckel said, "On this day many years ago I left you with Mr. and Mrs. Claus because I knew they could protect you."

Santa said, "You won't find more compassionate folk anywhere."

"Centuries before you were born, I saw a sign in the stars. The one to rescue the elves would be born in the far north."

"What sign did you see?"

"Do you know the stars?"

Santa said, "I watch them whenever I can."

"But do you know their names and meanings?"

Santa pointed to the blue star, and said, "Euchaia."

He pointed to a group of white stars, "The Captives."

Myckel nodded with satisfaction, "In the northern sky I saw the Morning Star face Beliach. Then the White Captives rose from Euchaia to meet him."

Santa raised his eyebrows, "And what should that have to do with me?"

"You were left to die on the pagan altar. When I saw that you were neither elf nor human, I took you to save you from Beliach, for I knew he would seek to destroy you. I brought you here and left you with a promise to your parents that I would return when you were of age." He paused and then, as if he had lingering doubts himself, said, "Some say that the prophesy is not true."

"What do you say about me?"

"You are the king of the elves to save us, foretold to be born on the night of the falling star." Myckel held out his arms, showing Santa the black rings around his wrists. "These rings keep us earthbound and enslaved to this darkness. We elves are immortal when the light of the stars are upon us, but here our lifeblood diminishes night-by-night. The time is drawing near for us. Our life-song is running out. Some of us are on the threshold of passing. We need to hear the stars sing again, to bask in their light, and to be with our maker the Morning Star."

"And how do you suppose I am to save you?"

At this, Myckel hesitated. "You must defeat Beliach. There is an abyss called the Deep of Balekhon. Where it leads, no one knows for certain, but it is said whoever enters will find himself in the remotest part of the heavens. You must cast him into the Deep. He will be held captive there every moment of every day except one: each year, from the time the sun rises to the time the sun sets on the date of his birth he will be free. But all the other elves will be free forever."

Santa took a deep breath and asked, "Where is your friend, Kintel? Does he not believe as you do that I am the king of the elves?"

"How do you know of Kintel?"

Santa replied, "The elves are not unknown to me."

Myckel shook his head, "I cannot speak for him."

"Bring him to me. I will be waiting for you tomorrow."

Santa's parents were eagerly awaiting him upon his return. He uttered not a word to them but put on his white cap and, tucking his pointy ears up underneath, lay down to sleep by the hearth. Fully grown, he was much too large for a tawdle house and therefore did not sleep in the upstairs loft with his family.

In the morning, he arose while everyone else was still fast asleep, and slipped outside. When they awoke, his poor parents thought he had gone away with Myckel, and his mother was in a terrible state of sobbing and sniffling when he walked through the door, his face flush with the cold. The twinkle in his eye was a little bit brighter than usual and he comforted his mother as well as he could, but it was no use. He could not assuage her fears. With a frightful degree of sincerity and pain on her face she asked him if he would be going away with the elf. He did not answer her directly. Instead, he said, "A friend is coming to see us. It might be that he holds the answer."

When the expected tap came on the door and Mr. Claus opened it, Myckel appeared and turned around to drag a mat into the house. Lying on the matt was the emaciated figure of Kintel. He was shivering to the bone. There were white husks where his eyes had been. In the years since Myckel and Kintel had delivered the babe to the Clauses, in the absence of the starlight, poor Kintel's life had drained from him. Santa came and looked down on the elf with compassion. "Do you think I am the king of the elves?"

Now blind and crippled, the creature replied in a faint voice, "I do not know who you are, sir. I have lost my sight. I know that the elves have been cursed and I am afraid we shall all die here if the Morning Star does not save us." Kintel's shivering was very sad to see, and his flesh was so pale that he seemed to be almost a vapor.

Santa knelt down and, as he drew nearer the suffering soul, his warmth seemed to ease Kintel's shuddering. He said, "Do not be afraid." Then he touched the elf on the forehead. There was something magic in his touch, for the life instantly returned to the soul and his eyes fluttered wide open. He leapt up, and with a look of happy, humble sincerity, knelt before Santa and enthusiastically exclaimed, "You are truly the king of the elves. Please accept my service, such as it is!"

Santa stepped back and gazed upon his mother. The spectacle of the sick elf had moved her deeply and she was suddenly overcome with the greatest measure of a mother's pride. "Oh come, come, Santa!" she cried, wrapping his tall form in a warm embrace. "If an elf king you must be, then an elf queen-mother I shall become!"

"Will you come lead us?" Myckel inquired with a tone of seriousness.

Santa pulled away from his mother and his glowing face softened, for there, standing in something of dread and wonder, was Linnea. She had seen the magical healing of the elf, Kintel, and its implications had immediately struck her. Her Santa was not meant only for her. He was indeed an elf as was rumored, and he was now displaying his allegiance. This frightened her, and her mind rapidly spiraled into one quick and heated emotion: she was angry. She made evident her sentiment with a flash of her eyes before whirling away and fleeing out the door.

And so Santa faced that great dilemma that every man must face at least once in his lifetime: to pursue or not to pursue. Santa pursued, and caught up with her in a matter of no time. He followed in her snow-steps several miles before she finally wearied and could go on no longer. When this happened, she simply crumpled into a heap and began sobbing. She did not know at this moment that the worst revelations were yet to come. But these revelations did not come from Santa himself, but from the elves.

Sensing that their stake in him was at risk, they had followed, and now emerged. Myckel was the wiser of the two in the ways of humans and he knew that it would be best if they allowed Santa to speak privately. Kintel, unfortunately, did not, and he interrupted their solitude with great vehemence, “Please, ma’am! Please! He is the king of the elves who was foretold would come to lead us to our freedom!” Then Kintel, in the most pitiable of fashions, got down on his knees, took the lady's hand most tenderly, and fervently implored her in the most compelling language to allow the Claus to take his place as the leader of the elves.

Kintel showed Linnea the rings around his and Myckel's wrists that kept them imprisoned and told of how they were unable to see the stars clearly or listen to their songs. He told her that surely this would continue until they would all wither away to mere whispers in the night. He told of the sorrow in their souls and the yearning they had for freedom.

Suddenly, much to everyone's alarm, Linnea cried, "IF YOU MUST!" They all stared at her with unease. "If you are the king of the elves, you must go and lead them, Santa. But I will not forsake you, not ever! I will wait for you here until the end!" Her earnest face, with cheeks flushed by the cold, looked to Santa with sadness—but her face was also brightened by that distinct and wondrous pleasure (commonly known these days as "Christmas Spirit") that one receives from knowing that he has done what was best for others and has not thought only of himself.

The twinkle in Santa's eye was so bright that it shined like a star as he enfolded her in his embrace.

When the party returned to the Claus residence, Mrs. Claus had already packed a bag with all the supplies one might require for a long journey. By the time they had eaten a last supper and were ready to depart, dusk had already stolen the light from the sky. Santa embraced all his family, including his older siblings. His mother bundled him in his new white coat. With his axe in his hand, he wished them all a very fond farewell and gave them this final, bittersweet declaration, “Love one and all, give gifts and do right. A merry morning to all, and to all a good night!” With that he closed the door and began his journey with the elves.

Chapter Four

They made very good progress from the Claus residence through the forest. As they walked among the giant cedars in the night, Myckel scoffed at Santa's choice of weapon, "An axe? Hardly a weapon befitting an elf."

"It is a weapon, but also a tool," Santa said.

"We should see the elves of Duzenfald. They can equip you properly."

"I do not require an elvish sword," Santa said. "My axe might one day save your life," Santa said. He suddenly stopped and said, "They're here."

"Who?"

Without answering, Santa crept forward. He led them towards a meadow where dappled shadows of moonlight played on the flowering grass. Santa called, "Friends, if you are willing, I need your help." The other elves saw no one.

Then, out of the darkness stepped an intimidating line of majestic reindeer. These were not the sort of reindeer one sees today, but were large—taller than a moose and stronger-built. With a voice deep and clear, the first and biggest deer spoke, "You know we are always here for you, Santa." The deer held his head high, his grand antlers towering above the meadow like a great, golden candelabrum.

Barely audibly, Myckel said, “I didn’t know.”

The chief deer said, “Didn’t know there were talking reindeer in these woods?” He nodded, “Humans are as quick to kill talking reindeer as they are walking elves.”

The elves and the deer closed the distance between them, neither making a sound. The stately deer said, “We have seen Dark Elves of Beliach in these woods. They are searching for you.”

Santa nodded, “All the more important, then, that we pass through quickly. I have need of your aid, and this time it is no small favor.”

“You have helped us many times when we were in need. A true friend is there in both times of joy and of trouble. We are at your service.”

“We make our way south to Balekhon. We would be most indebted if your swift hooves conveyed us as far as the sea of Sevant.”

In response, the chief deer knelt low before Santa, followed by all his herd.

Having no experience riding anything, the elves awkwardly swayed from side to side as they sat astride the deer. Santa, however, was quite steady, coolly resting his hands upon his thighs.

Kintel, for his part, found the experience fascinating. He could hear the animal’s heavy breathing and see the white puffs it made in the cold night air. Trying to be sociable, he asked his deer if he had lived long in these woods, but the beast simply snorted in response.

Suddenly, Myckel said, "Stop! I hear a voice!" No one else heard this voice, but Myckel explained, "It is Dryrie! She asks us to wait. She is coming to join us."

And wait they did, for hours and hours while the deer became increasingly impatient, stamping their hooves and pawing at the ground. The chief deer, whose name was Roatark, warned, "We must be wary of the Dark Elves. We cannot linger for long."

"Myckel?" Santa said.

"She shouldn't be long."

"Has she spoken to you since?"

"It is unwise to say much between such distance. The Dark Elves can use their dark magic to capture what is spoken in secret."

At length, the sky was thickened with clouds, and cold winds began to creak and sway the giant cedars. A fierce and biting snow fell, and the deer huddled together for warmth.

With no sight nor sound of Dryrie, they waited, and how they survived the freezing winds and snow I cannot say, but just when they were about to lose hope, they saw a strange light glowing through the thick of the snowfall.

“The Dark Elves?” Roatark questioned in a foreboding voice.

“We must be ready for the worst,” Santa said.

“On your guard!” Roatark commanded his kinsman.

As the light drew near, Myckel cried in uncharacteristic excitement, “Dryrie!” for it was she, holding a torch of everlasting flame. Upon her arrival, Dryrie told Santa, perched as he was atop the imposing reindeer, “I don’t believe that you are the king of the elves. I come for the sake of my friends, Myckel and Kintel.”

With the icy snow swirling around him and a white frost formed on his beard, Santa said, “I am not a tyrant, Dryrie. But I am your king. I hope that, for now, you will at least count me among your friends.”

Dryrie nodded acknowledgement.

Jaylit, on the other hand, exclaimed that he wholeheartedly believed that Santa was the elf king.

Riding the deer, the elves made swift progress over the increasingly mountainous terrain. They reached a frozen river which coursed down the rocks like a stream of glass. The deer followed this, skillfully finding their footing on the boulders and jagged outcrops until they came upon an icy pool where a solid crystal waterfall spilled from a mighty plateau.

Myckel dismounted, saying, "The elves of Duzenfald are the greatest forgers of steel the world has ever seen. Your axe will be a forgotten memory once you see one, Santa."

Myckel led the elves behind the frozen waterfall and into the darkness of a tunnel. With the brush of her hand, Dryrie lit her torch with a blue flame.

"Have any of you been to the Elven City of Duzenfald before?" Myckel asked, to which he received a negative response. "They began digging these tunnels when men launched the great persecution against the elves."

The stone was marred by countless gouges from pickaxes, and the ceiling was blackened with soot. A large stone blocked all but a narrow gap in the tunnel, and each elf had to squeeze himself through. Beyond this, the way was thickly impeded by spears that had been thrust down through holes in the ceiling. Myckel tried to squeeze his way between them but found he could not.

Santa held up his axe and offered, "Perhaps my primitive axe might be of some use."

Myckel stepped aside and allowed Santa to put his weapon to work. The blade was so sharp that it cleanly sliced through each pole with a single strike. When at last they made it through the poles, they came to a pile of collapsed stones. There was only a thin opening at the top of these through which the elves could pass by worming their way on their stomachs.

When at last they had squeezed through and were dusting themselves off, Dryrie held up the torch so they could see. They were in a large chamber with blackened, round walls and ceiling. Visible through patches where the soot was thin were spellbinding mosaic scenes of natural wonders: forests, waterfalls, and animals.

The floor was littered with the charred remains of wooden furniture and, strewn among the ashes, beautifully crafted goblets, pitchers, and swords of silver and gold. There were also glass ornaments of the greatest beauty: animals real and fanciful, elves, and designs which looked like the most intricate of snowflakes.

Shaking his head in disbelief, Myckel said, “What happened here?”

Lifting one of the goblets, Dryrie said, “Everything burned.”

A wide entrance with a downward ramp invited them deeper into the subterranean labyrinth, and they followed this through to a branching passage. One had a staircase leading down, and this they followed. The stairs were rounded, each step carefully and painstakingly chiseled from the stone. The staircase took a meandering route, sometimes spiraling, sometimes straight, but always deeper and deeper into the darkness. The acrid smell of burnt ruins grew increasingly thick in their nostrils the farther they went, and the soot became heavier on the walls. Branching off from the corridor were more round tunnels and round rooms, all of them decorated with beautiful mosaics of minute glass beads glazed by ash and soot. Myckel peered into each, but found them all blackened by fire, whatever furniture was in them now nothing more than fragments of coal and gray powder. In one room were several large, gaping holes in the floor. Myckel said, "The wine distillery." He walked to a window that looked into blackness. Dryrie followed him and pushed the torch through, revealing a wide and seemingly endless shaft of shining silver, with openings spiraling all the way down. "This was made to provide starlight. Elves can survive a siege here longer than the lifetimes of their attackers. But I feel no starlight here. Whoever attacked this place knew of this weakness, and must have packed it at the top." He called, "Is anyone here?" His voice echoed down the chute, lost to the interminable black depth.

In a low voice, Santa said, "Be wary. There might be enemies in these depths."

"If there are, they already know where we are," Myckel sharply retorted.

Myckel led them ever lower, passing tunnel after tunnel and room after room. The air grew cooler.

Finally, they reached the base of the stairs where there was a small, bare hollow. Here the walls were ornamented with visions of galaxies and planets and stars. Myckel brushed some of the dirt from one of the mosaics, revealing a seascape with towering, orange waves illuminated by two moons. "These were made before the elves' existence among the stars was memory. Now, it is only myth." He pushed on the wall with both hands and, with a loud grating sound, it shifted. He pushed harder and harder and the wall spun, revealing a vast, cavernous space. They stepped inside and stared up in awe. Overlooking the cavern were many walkways and dark openings like a city of windows looking in. The hall was so large that giant, round pillars supported the weight of its lofty ceiling. Torches burning in various shades of warm light shone from patterned notches that formed arches and crosses of light, and the walls were all of the brightest silver.

"This, this is the true Secret Elven City of Duzenfald. Everything above was a mere trick and shadow of this."

The sprawling floor was blanketed in a thick layer

of ash and charred ruins. As they walked among these, Myckel sadly shook his head.

"Oh, no!" Dryrie cried. "It can't be!"

Many of the charred shells were not of furniture at all, but were the remains of all the elves who had perished there. Some were on their hands and knees, some covered their eyes, some lay in tender embraces, some cowered with their feet tucked under their bodies, and others lay with their mouths gaping in silent screams of anguish. As the elves looked across the immense space, they were filled with heavy grief. The number of their fallen kinsman was vast.

Kintel stood before an ashy figure whose arm was outstretched as if to reach for the hand of a rescuer who never came. His tears flowed freely as he asked, "Who would do this?"

Myckel said low, "It is the Dark Elves. Only they could have known of this place."

Santa lifted a lustrous, black orb that looked like polished onyx from where it sat among the ashes. Having closely studied it, he said, "Dark magic is at work here. Beliach would destroy all the elves who do not follow him—if we allow it."

Myckel said, "Then you must finish him before it is too late!"

Santa raised his eyebrows and said, "You have not the good of the elves in mind but your own vengeance."

"You are correct," Myckel seethed. "Kelia was there the day Beliach stepped foot on Euchaia. She saw him, and he knew she would be an everlasting witness to his crime. I heard her cry my name as he tore her wings off her back and stifled her life song." He bitterly cast his eyes to the ground, "I was not strong enough to defeat him." His eyes rose to meet Santa's, "But you are."

"You say this only because you saw what I did at Bannonith."

Myckel, his face filled with awe, asked, "How do you know I was there?"

"I saw you hiding in the tree."

"You could not have seen me. I made sure of that."

"No elf is hidden from me," Santa said. "You watched as the Dark Elves secured the chains of the people, and yet you did nothing."

"Men and their troubles are no concern of mine."

"The fate of the world rests on those who make the concerns of others their own." Santa dropped the orb. It landed in the dust, sending a plume of ash into the air.

The elves, at length, climbed the long tunnel back up to the surface and emerged from behind the waterfall to find the deer waiting for them.

"Hurry!" Roatark exclaimed, "The wolves are

coming!”

Chapter Five

The deer's ears pricked and they nervously stamped as a distant howl echoed in the night. The elves leaped into the trees and dropped onto the backs of the deer, who sprung down the hill with such long, arcing leaps and so much speed as to make the elves afraid they should be cast off and dashed to pieces on the boulders.

Kintel clung to his deer's fur with all the strength he could muster. He was violently jostled and the frigid wind mercilessly whipped him. But he held all the tighter when the deer reached the top of a ridge and, in the hollow below, Kintel caught glimpse of a pack of large, black wolves adorned by prominent, furry manes around their shoulders like regal coats. The wolves rapidly tore their way up the hill, snarling and barking with fiercely confident gleams in their eyes. Their canine teeth were not of the sort possessed by any wolf or dog with which you or I are familiar, but were long, curved, and pointed like the teeth of a saber-tooth cat.

Roatark shouted, "Make for the Gorge of Malach!"

With terrifying speed and agility, the deer flew along the top of the ridge, veering right and left to avoid the pine trunks. The wolves quickly overtook them, but due to the vertical rise of the ridge, could merely nip at their hooves from below. Kintel could scarcely believe it when he heard the rumbling voice of his deer from underneath him say, "Hold on!" There was, of course, no need for the admonition because Kintel was already holding on so tightly that his knuckles hurt. At any rate, he wouldn't have had time to react because, abruptly following it, he saw the ground fall underneath them as the deer took a flying leap off the ridge and over the heads of the ferocious wolves.

Kintel almost dropped to the ground like an untethered bag when the deer landed with a great thump and resumed his gallop. With the wolves hard upon them, the deer charged through the forest, panting with great heaving breaths and foaming at their mouths. Just as the wolves were snapping for their legs, the deer bolted onto a plain that was layered in deep snow. With the wolves struggling to bound over the trapping snow, the deer quickly put distance between themselves and their growling pursuers. There were no trees or bushes to stop brutal winds from lifting the snow up in blinding sheets and flurries.

The deer lessened their speed, gulping for air, but Roatark commanded, "Don't slow down!" Just as he said this, he gasped and stumbled. Regaining his footing, he slackened his gait, and coughed.

"What is it?" Santa asked, putting a hand to the burdened beast's neck.

But Roatark said nothing and Santa and the other elves quickly realized that two long, black arrows had pierced his flank.

"The Dark Elves!" Myckel shouted. "They'll be poisoned!"

"Don't stop!" Roatark roared. "To the gorge!" To the shock of the companions, he vaulted forward in a remarkable show of strength.

Though they looked for them through the white screen of snow, they couldn't find the Dark Elves who had fired the arrows. They heard the barking of the wolves, however, and raced through the fury of the wind. The reindeer somehow knew the way, though nothing could be seen but the billowing curtain of snow.

Roatark began to trip and cough, but he didn't stop and hardly slowed, though he did fall a little behind his kinsman.

A female deer called back in an alarmed voice, "Roatark!"

Roatark responded, "Go on, Thrushti!"

When at last the deer galloped out of the great white blizzard and into a clear and moonlit flatland, the wolves were nearly upon them. Ahead the land abruptly ended in a seemingly bottomless cliff. Far across a great chasm was an opposing cliff, the trees that topped it so small and distant as to appear as mere bushes.

“We’re trapped!” Myckel shouted.

“Trust the deer!” Santa replied from behind, astride Roatark. The deer lowered their antlers and charged forward, drawing the last reserves of their strength. The wolves, now with little snow to contend with, snapped at their legs, growling quite fearsomely. The deer kicked at them with their hooves and managed to hit two of them in their muzzles, sending them yelping and toppling to the ground.

All the reindeer except Roatark reached the cliff edge and, mightily thrusting their hind legs, sailed into the air like the seagulls on a cliff of the coast. Just as Roatark was about to reach the edge, a wolf leaped up and clamped its teeth onto one of the black arrow shafts. With a potent kick, Roatark majestically soared off the cliff-face. Santa let forth a mighty shout, raising his axe above his own head as they flew across the immense gorge where, meandering like a little trail of ants below, was the course of a black river. He blunted the wolf, sending it tumbling through the air down the gorge.

From the other side, the deer who had already completed the jump stood anxiously watching Roatark and Santa, doubtful that Roatark’s waning strength was enough. But Roatark's hooves thundered upon the ground and he tripped, with Santa leaping off as Roatark's muscular body toppled over. Santa, having rolled over the ground and now in a heap, stood to his feet. But Roatark remained fallen. Thrushti anxiously trotted to his side, crying "Roatark!" in a voice all but trembling with fear.

The arrow shafts were shifting with his labored breaths. "Thrushti," said the great reindeer, "You must take our friends to the sea."

"But not without you!" Thrushti pitifully protested.

"This," Roatark said, nodding with his antlers towards Santa, "is the king of the Elves and the one to save them. Time is running short. You must—" he coughed. "You must take them."

Kintel would not have believed it possible had he not seen it, but a tear fell from Thrushti's muzzle and froze in the snow. She nuzzled her husband's nose with hers, closing her eyes. So, too, did Roatark close his, and the arrow shafts were still, like flagstaffs without banners or masts without sails: black, stark, and lifeless.

An arrow just like those which had impaled Roatark suddenly pierced a nearby tree. Though very small in the great distance across the chasm, visible on the edge of the opposing cliff were mysterious, hooded figures that stood among the pacing wolves.

Dryrie speedily nocked her bow and sent an arrow towards them, but it failed to reach even halfway across the gorge.

"It is the Dark Elves," Myckel grimly said. "Black magic is at work to propel these arrows. We must hurry. Arrows like these rarely fail to find their target."

Thrushti raised her graceful neck to glare with terrible wrath at the dark figures on the other side.

"Thrushti!" Myckel called.

Reluctantly she turned, and they hurried into the shelter of the woods.

Sad and silent was the journey to the coast of the foaming Sea of Sevant. When at last they reached it, nary a word was spoken, but the elves hugged the thick, furred necks of their newfound friends before they stepped out onto the water.

The gray waves were monstrous indeed and crashed against the rocks with horrible menace. Despite the ferociousness of the sea, the elves and their king were able to walk upon it. Elves, you see, can tread upon water just as naturally as they can upon land. On stormy seas, though, their actions are more akin to clambering than walking, and this is what they were forced to do. From the peak of an immense ocean wave, they waved back at their companions, the deer. With their heads held high and their majestic antlers adorning them like great and regal crowns, they bowed low to the king of the elves.

Their journey across the Sea of Sevant was not free from dreadful peril. After several days, the monstrous form of a fearsome black whale burst out from the sea before them while others sprayed from their blow-holes behind.

With hungry whales surrounding them, the elves made a leap between two of them to chance an escape. The whales pursued, leaping out from the waves at intervals with their mouths open wide and their teeth poised to snap. Santa stopped to give a great whistle (for what purpose no one could then guess), and while he was doing so a great spew of spray ruptured from directly underneath Dryrie, sending her body flipping into the air like a rag doll. When she landed, the giant mouth of the most ferocious of the whales took hold of her leg and dragged her under the surface. With the chaotic sprays and leaps from the whales all around, Myckel shouted in horror.

Santa tossed his cap and axe to a dismayed Kintel and dove into the water, disappearing from sight. All at once, all the whales withdrew from the surface, leaving a bewildered Myckel, Kintel and Jaylit alone. As the terrible seconds became terrible minutes, Kintel said, “hope Dryrie has not drowned already!”

Myckel did not speak, but stood with his arms

crossed. Then, with such a great bellow and such a great crash as the elves had never heard before, the enormous form of a gray-skinned whale nearly the size of a mountain split the sea in two, carrying all the scrambling elves with it up into the air. Water cascaded off the sides of the beast like waterfalls. But there, perched right on the front of its forehead, was Santa holding the limp frame of Dryrie.

The smaller whales began an attack on the gigantic one, but then fled when the latter, in a single swift motion, scooped three of them in his mouth and crunched them to pieces.

With the danger quite gone, Santa lay Dryrie down on the soft skin of the giant beast. When Kintel saw how many ways in which her little body was shattered, his brave heart was broken and he burst into tears. Myckel said with no small hint of malice in his tone, "Had you called for the gray whale sooner, this would not have happened."

Santa silently raised his glistening eyes to Myckel, but did not return the challenge. He then lowered to his knees and touched Dryrie on the forehead. And, just as with Kintel, something magical happened and she breathed a deep breath. He helped her to her feet.

Seeing Santa dripping wet and the other two staring at her with amazement, she quickly surmised the situation. But rather than thanking her rescuer, her eyes mysteriously filled with tears and she looked down to her feet, as if in shame.

"Why are your eyes downcast?" Santa asked her.

"I did not believe you were the king."

Touching her chin, he lifted her countenance, "Do not let your heart be troubled. You believed in the promise of the Morning Star, didn't you?"

She nodded, blinking hopefully.

"Then likewise trust me, Dryrie. You will see greater things than this."

During the rest of their journey across the sea, they at times stopped and, lit "forever" fires for warmth or to roast up some fish for Santa (as he was the only one among them who required food—elves do not eat as you or I, but use the light of stars for energy). At length, the clouds parted and they basked in the light of the stars. As they lay on their backs staring up at the glistening night sky, there was no sound to interrupt the stillness and the stars in all their sparkling glory almost seemed to be at their fingertips.

Kintel asked, "Do you really believe we will fly to the stars again, Santa?"

"You will, indeed. You will find your wings and you will find rest in the splendor of the heavens. You will be wanting for nothing, filled and overflowing with the light of the stars. The Morning Star who made you will free you from all cares and troubles, and you will live in his light forever."

Jaylit questioned, "How do you know this?"

"I can see it."

This respite in the clouds was brief, unfortunately, and the remainder of their trip across the sea was not so pleasantly memorable, and was rather characterized by freezing sleet and icy winds. Thus it was with great relief that they finally spied the rocky shore and, beyond that, the magnificent Mountains of Ashet, their snow-white peaks gleaming in the sunlight against the blue backdrop of the boundless horizon.

Upon reaching the shore and mounting the rocky hillside, the party reached at last the grassy foothills of the Ashet Mountains. Knowing that the route ahead through the cliffs and ice would be treacherous, indeed, and that they would need all the strength they could muster for its passage, they stopped to rest and admire the majesty of the peaks. While the climbing would be difficult, they knew that nothing compared to the fear that gripped those who encountered the creatures that lurked in the crevasses and waited to seek some passing innocents whose frozen corpses could be stored away to be withdrawn later for razor-sharp teeth to crush to little bits and pieces as a savory frosty feast in the dark of some night.

Chapter Six

A murleith, you see, is a very nasty creature, with eyes so blood-red and bodies so death-white that you'd feel its icy grip on you sooner than you'd see its sharp claw reaching for you. Because their eyes were so noticeable in the snow, the murleith hunted with their eyes closed and spread their webbed hands out to feel for the thaw of any poor warm-blooded creature. Most of the time, the murleith fed on mountain goats, but delightful to them was the rare occasion when they could stick the long claws of both hands onto the flesh of something smarter or more difficult to catch. Murleith breaths were so cold that they could turn flesh to solid ice, so after they captured their prey, they would shackle its hands and legs and wait for the rest of it to freeze.

I must tell you that Kintel had never been so afraid as the time that he was scaling a cliff with his bare hands and waiting for the murleith to suddenly slip out of some crack and send him tumbling down to the treacherous depths below. Their only comfort was the rugged beauty of the sharp, magnificent peaks high above them, shrouded by wisps of cloud and looking almost as if the stone had been a violently churning sea that had suddenly stopped still in its place, to be relentlessly whittled away under the buffeting winds and snows of the ages.

When the group reached a ledge that had enough room for them to pause for a respite, they did so, with Jaylit proposing that they light a fire. Darkness was closing in, and the air which was before cold, had now numbed their faces and toes, but Myckel spoke with a low voice, "I should not light a fire if I were you."

Jaylit paused, seeming agitated, "Why ever not?"

"They are attracted by warmth."

Jaylit shrugged his shoulders, "If we don't light a fire we'll all freeze to death."

Myckel raised his brows, "As you wish, but just remember that the light of the fire won't make it any easier to see them. They are concealed by any light."

When Jaylit had awoken the flames with the brush of his hand, they gathered around in a circle, sitting down to warm themselves. As they gazed into the beauty of the blaze, a deep and heavy weariness fell upon them. One by one, their eyelids drooped until they could hold them up no longer.

Two spots of blood-red glinted in the moonlight high above them. They disappeared and reappeared, each time nearer than before. Then, as two black sets of long claws reached out above each of the elves, a thick stick suddenly landed in the fire, causing a great spray of sparks that rest upon the murleith, exposing them in all their ghastly repulsiveness. The elves woke with a terrible start just in time to see the murleith slinking up the cliff in flight, their bony white arms effortlessly lifting them higher and higher until they vanished into a chasm.

A large party of dwarves suddenly appeared, armed with axes and spears and clothed with huge belts and chainmail. Their beards were thick and long, and their hair was untamed, except for the leader, whose blond locks were braided all the way down to his waist. They gripped perfectly round shield which they used to great effect, banging and clanging them together with shouts and vehement threats, to surround and press the elves to the very edge of the ice-cliff.

When it was quite apparent that one more step by the dwarves could send the whole company of elves off the cliff, the lead dwarf, with a great deal more gold in his armor and with a longer beard than the others shouted, "Why are ye passing through our mountains?"

Myckel said, "Our travel is none of your concern. You don't own these mountains!"

"No?" the dwarf said. He smiled and chuckled to his companions, "They think that these are not our mountains!" The dwarves joined him in laughter. To one of this kinsman, the dwarf said, "What say ye, brother Bompus? Since these be not our mountains, I wonder whose mountains they be?"

Bompus, with great amusement replied, "Beliach's, I'd fancy a guess?"

The chief dwarf frowned as he said to the elves, "Your elven leader Beliach's arm has grown long, indeed. He commands that any elves caught passing through here are to be apprehended." With a terrible glare, the dwarf commanded, "Lay down yer arms or you'll be seein' the bottom of the cliff."

Santa's heavy axe landed on the ice with a clink.

Myckel protested, "Don't be so foolish, Santa. They will sell us to Beliach! Dwarves value gold over life!"

"Myckel," said Santa in a tone which demanded obedience, "lay down your sword."

Grudgingly, the elf obeyed, followed by the others.

Looking at Santa, the chief dwarf commented, "An elf with an axe. Never seen that afore, have ye, lads?"

His dwarf companions agreed, with Bompus saying, "Nay, brother Dantor! N'er and a day!"

Dantor said, "Ye might be an elf I could take kindly to, assuming ye be sensible in other matters."

"What other matters?" Santa asked.

"Takin' direction. Now go!"

The dwarves outnumbered the elves five to one. If

not for this, the elves probably would have chanced an escape. But as it was, the dwarves said nothing as they pushed the elves through clefts and along thin shelves of rock that, at points, had only enough room for one foot at a time. The dwarves, like fat little mountain goats, were quite sprightly and lithe as they skipped and jumped from rock to rock.

At length, the trail took them downwards, towards the vast forest on the other side of the mountain range. The dwarves became palpably more spirited as they walked, and when they entered a giant crevasse in a glacier, the sides of which were glassy and blue and beautiful, they forsook any discretion which they had thus far exhibited and began to noisily chatter amongst themselves (mostly boasts about their ore and their tools and their weapons). The crevasse narrowed above them until they were entirely encased in an icy, blue tunnel. At this juncture, the dwarves took up a song, their merry voices echoing off the crystalline walls.

Elves, elves, too many came!
One's too many; they're all the same!

Not a lot and not a few.
So many elves, what shall we do?

Pack them up and bring them down,
down to the deep to meet the Crown.

What will he think? What will he say?
"Chop off their heads! Take them away!"

The cheerful song ended when they came to an abrupt termination in the tunnel where solid rock blocked the way. But this was no ordinary rock. It was smooth as glass, polished so finely that Dantor's reflection shone on it as he approached. He uttered not a word, but the stone suddenly shifted, sliding straight down as if the ground had given way underneath it and it was dropping into the mountain. But then a top lip appeared, exposing a perfectly straight tunnel hewn from rock. Lining the tunnel were a series of torches set neatly on the walls in golden sconces shaped like the horns of rams. One of the dwarves hopped through the opening into the tunnel before another stone slid down from the top, blocking the way again.

And so it went, with stones giving way to gaps over and over again, that each dwarf jumped through and each elf was pushed through until all were on the other side. The stones stopped shifting and the entrance was once again blocked.

The tunnel was not very long, and at the end was

a black opening through which could be glimpsed a shaft of undeterminable depth. The dwarves stood patiently at the opening as if they had suddenly lost all sense of where they were or where they were going. But then a golden cage with detailed embellishments and an intricately woven carpet descended and, with a loud clang and a shudder, stopped. A system of copious gears and springs whirred and clacked, causing a sturdy wire door to drop open across the gap between the cage and the tunnel—like a little drawbridge.

The cage was of such large capacity that, after the last dwarf and the last elf was in, a second party of dwarves and elves could have easily followed.

Dantor lifted a well-greased lever with the tip of his finger. With the same clickety-clack whir of the mechanism, the little drawbridge raised up and the cage started to descend, creaking and swaying a little as it did. The stone walls on all sides flew by with increasing speed until the sound of the air squeezing through the gaps on the sides of the cage was as loud as the gale of a violent storm. The air was heavier the deeper they descended, and descend they did, for so long and with such speed that Kintel became thoroughly convinced they were traveling to the very center of the earth.

Finally, the cage slowed with a reverberating

whine and they heard the echoes of clinks and clangs and huffs and rumbles coming up the shaft. The walls of the shaft fell away to reveal a tunnel of cavernous proportions. Scattered everywhere like an army of ants were dwarves engaged in all kinds of labor. On ledges, in holes, on scaffolds, and manning large machinations with assemblies of giant gears and levers and billows: the dwarves were everywhere. They wielded picks and anvils, hammers and mallets, and chisels and files. Most of them were shirtless, the sweat from their labor glistening on their tubby abdomens. Mules taller than the dwarves were yoked to the spokes of giant wheels which they turned by walking. Channels in the stone and golden aqueducts conveyed water to steaming pools and giant waterwheels. There were enormous heaps of stone cut or crushed, having been dumped there from carts that rode tracks on rock ledges above. This great spectacle was illuminated by torches which were everywhere they could possibly be: on posts, hung from cables, and in cracks and crannies in the rock-faces.

Dangling from a thick rope which slowly bounced up and down, the cage passed over this great manifestation of industry. One dwarf stopped to look up at the cage and shouted, "Did ye catch anything?"

"Aye!" shouted back Dantor. "Elves!"

"The master will be none too pleased to hear that!"

"Nay," eagerly chuckled the dwarf. "A right fit he'll have, no doubt!"

The dwarves all found this highly amusing, their beady little dwarf eyes glinting at the elves from under dark and bushy brows.

The cage entered a small tunnel before dipping down into a huge cavern. A vast lake filled the base of this, and shimmering on its surface was the sparkling reflection of what stood in the middle glowing and resplendent like a celestial city floating on the water: a cluster of innumerable structures with heights ranging in size (but larger in the center) and lit with innumerable torches. Brass pipes protruded from the flat roofs of each of the buildings. These connected to larger brass pipes and these to even larger pipes until there was but one thick pipe which was carried on a series of tresses across the water and into the stone of the cavern wall.

The cage lightly came to rest on four stone pillars and the door fell open. A stone staircase led down to a wharf on the water where several longboats were moored. The faint din of voices and claps and clangs and clamors echoed across the lake, but clearer was the sound of the water lapping against the pier.

"Tell me now, elf," Dantor said. "Do ye still think this isn't our mountain?"

Meckel responded not, but was willingly led into one of the longboats. There were rows of benches and, at the foots of these, metal slots into which the dwarves sipped their feet. Dantor gave the command and they all began pedaling. The sound of trickling water came from the rear of the vessel where a dwarf manned a rudder, and in no time the boat was making a speedy crossing towards the center of the lake. A breeze humid but pleasantly cool whipped the dwarves' hair and beards.

The closer they came, the sooner they saw that the buildings were very tightly compacted except where lanes for boats divided them. Wood beams layered in gold leaf supported them and stones either chiseled, crushed, or mixed into mortar made up the walls. They were quaint and charming, with glowing windows overlooking the water—though except for several which were made entirely of meticulously sculpted stone, they were inelegant and imprecise, leaning into one another like idle children. The buildings had no roofs, but were rimmed on their tops by wooden walkways with shiny bronze balustrades and thick woven ropes laced with gold. At the center of these walkways were buildings that looked like they had been dropped onto the buildings below them. On top of these were more skywalks and more structures, with catwalks connecting all the buildings across the gaps. The effect was such that the place on the whole looked like a collection of giant layered cakes of metal, wood, and stone.

Busy dwarves in all manner of dress were carried by the hasty patter of their big dwarf feet over the walkways and under bridges and down staircases and over roofs. They greeted one another, tipped their hats, and cheerfully tugged the beards of those they bumped into. The dwarves in dresses had beards just as thick as the dwarves in pants, but their cheeks were a quite a bit rosier.

The boat passed down a waterway between structures, with the elves gaping up at the bustle and activity high above in the footbridges. Aside from the occasional rug-beater or bearded dwarf child peeping out, there was little activity in the windows lower down.

The boat eased softly through the watercourse until it intersected with a larger one. Here, the dwarf manning the rudder made a sharp turn, and ahead was a large and stately-looking stone building with a shining domed roof. A queue of uncharacteristically desponded dwarves led all the way around the building and then some. There was no particular pattern to this population, with the same variety of dwarves present as could be seen doing business among the roof-tops, though there were at least two mothers holding bearded little infants with large eyes peeping out from under their bushy eyebrows.

The dwarves docked the boat and led their elf prisoners directly up to the entrance, demanding that the waiting dwarves part to give them passage to the doors. As they obliged, some of the queued dwarves shouted insults at the elves.

In short order the elves found themselves in an expansive polished-stone hall that looked very much like a library—with books lining every wall. Dantor bowed before a plump and very short dwarf with an extremely elegant mustache and meticulously braided beard who sat upon a monumental throne. With cushions that were much too big for him, it appeared that he struggled not to slide off at every moment. He was dressed more like a broker than a king, however, with neatly pressed trousers and a buttoned vest. He wore no crown. Dantor said, “We caught these elves in the pass, King Bufus.”

“In the pass, ye say?” King Bufus said, hopping off his seat and eyeing the elves with disdain. He threw up his hands in despair, “No, no! Not more elves! Whatever shall we do? ’Tis as if they’re pouring out of the rocks! I’ve done my part, I’ve done what can be done, but we’re not running a charity. We’re running a robust and diversified kingdom! Have ye any idea the challenge it is to move the attitude of an entire people from a mindless fixation on a handful of commodities—the value of which rises and falls at the whims of supply and demand—to a stable exchange of a plurality of goods and services? Well, we are at the crux of just such a transformation, and let me assure ye it has been no small success! The kingdom of the Ashet Dwarves has never been more prosperous. But we won't be for long if these detestable, destitute elves keep knocking down our doors!" Then, looking to Myckel, he said, "Say, whence ye hail?"

"We are elves of the north."

"Duzenfald?"

"No, the wilderlands."

"And what be yer business?"

Santa said, "I am the king of the elves."

Blinking in surprise, the king shuffled over to him and brought his face up as high as he could to look at him closely, "*You* are the king of the elves?" He gave a chuckle, "The elves have no king. They are divided and leaderless." Stepping up to his large seat, King Bufus said, "These are the last days of the elves. I fear they shall very soon be no more."

Before the dwarf king could say more, a very frightened-looking dwarf rushed in from the door, "King Bufus the Prodigious! Dark elves have come! They insist upon an immediate congress with your highness!"

“How immediate?” asked the flustered king.

“Right the way!”

“Oh!” the king moaned in distress. “This comes at a most inopportune time.” He flitted his hand, “Hurry, hide our guests!”

And with that the elves were speedily whisked away through another set of doors into a great dining room. Huddled together, they peeped through a crack between the doors.

The hall seemed to fill with an overpowering darkness as tall figures in black cloaks strode inside. Their movements were graceful and yet somehow extremely aggressive.

The dwarf king tried to speak, but one of the Dark Elves raised his hand and interrupted with a voice strong and confident, “Word has reached us of a troupe of elves passing through these mountains. Your watchmen wouldn’t have apprehended them, would they?”

“Elves, say ye?” the king blustered, beads of sweat glistening on his forehead. Looking to Dantor, he said, “Had ye seen an elf, ye’d have seized it, wouldn’t ye?”

“Aye,” Dantor said with a grin. “And yoked it to our mule team.”

“No elves, here, as you see,” King Bufus assured, “exceptin’ yerselves, of course.”

In a voice filled with disdain, the Dark Elf said,

"We are no longer known as elves. We live among men, as men. The elves," he spit the words out, "are a dying race. Beliach wishes to be sure of that. Any elves who will not convert are to be destroyed. You know he has a great and formidable power." The Dark Elf turned his hood to look around the hall as he said, "You have such a prosperous kingdom under the mountain. It would be a terrible loss should it come to ruin."

"A terrible loss, indeed," said the king, "and one which we are very much eager to avoid."

The elf looked directly at King Bufus, "Then be doubly certain your loyalty to Beliach's cause cannot come into question."

"Rest assured our loyalty increases every day. We consider it an accretive asset!"

"Very well. We leave you with a parting gift: a small demonstration of Beliach's power." With the flick of his hand, the Dark Elf cast a shiny round orb like onyx to the floor. It rolled, coming to rest in a groove between stones. The Dark Elf, in perfect synchronicity with his kinsman, turned around and walked towards the door.

As soon as the door slammed shut, an inky, wispy black smoke like the luxuriant tresses of a woman's hair began to stream from the orb, and an ear-splitting, shrieking sound filled the hall. This cloud of smoke, once fully discharged, appeared to move entirely of its own accord, snaking and curling about the hall until it touched upon Bompus and entered his body.

What it did to him is too horrible to put into words, but when it was finished, he was nothing more than a smoldering statue of embers, first glowing golden yellow, then fading to gray ash.

Crying his brother's name in a voice barren and broken, Dantor hurried to the figure of soot and stared, face to face, into its lifeless eyes. "No, Bompus! Nooo!" His beady dwarven eyes brimming with tears, he turned to the king, "What have they done? We must stop them!" He drew his sword from its sheath, spinning around for the doors.

But the king said, "Dantor, ye mustn't do this! They'll kill us all!"

Dantor stopped, his head hanging low.

"Ye saw what they can do to one man. Think of what they could do to the whole city! We have peace and we have life, but it is ever so fragile. 'Tis merely because we do not challenge their authority that they let us be!"

"But it's me brother they've killed!" Dantor said, quite pathetically.

"I know," King Bufus said, drawing near to the downtrodden dwarf. "A warrior and a hero. His death has meaning—a sacrifice for all. Don't lose that meaning by bringing death to everyone, I beg ye."

Dantor slowly dropped to his knees, his sword clanging on the polished stone floor, and he wailed his fallen brother's name, a long and horrible sound that echoed off the rock and faded into oblivion. Then, drawing his breath, he cast a dark eye towards the dining room where the elves were hidden. "It's these elves! They brought this upon us! Why must we protect them? Our kingdom will be a ruin because of them!"

King Bufus said, "A kingdom without justice is no kingdom at all. The elves have done us no wrong. It is only just and right that we protect them."

At these words, Myckel pushed open the doors and said, "We ask not to be protected! We wish only to be on our way!"

King Bufus said, "Ye are not the elves of whom he speaks."

"Then of whom does he speak?"

Grimly, the king said to Dantor, "Let us take them to the ancient mines. If that one is indeed their king, perhaps he can solve our problem."

Chapter Seven

As they left the great building, the people waiting for an audience with King Bufus dropped to their knees before him. Dantor declared, "The king will be acceptin' no further audience today! Bring yer concerns at the morrow!"

All the dwarves let out a collective sigh of dismay before beginning to disperse.

The party of elves and dwarves walked to the dock and boarded the longboat. Some dwarves on the dock lowered two heavy chests into the hull, causing the boat to sink deeper into the water. Then they sat in silence as the vessel slipped down the channel, between the buildings, and into the lake.

With no wind to stir it, the lake was as still as glass. The longboat slid over the water smoothly, scarcely denting the surface. The dwarves steered for an enormous, triangular entrance to a dark tunnel. Upon entering the tunnel, Dantor lit a lamp. The only sounds that could be heard were the soft whir of the mechanical system by which the craft was propelled and the faint ripples of the water.

At the end of the tunnel was a crisply cut stone ledge where they moored the boat. Dantor leaped onto the ledge and ran his fingers along the stone wall for some distance, apparently feeling for some aberration in its smooth surface. This he finally found, for he pushed on the wall and a cylindrical piece gave way. At exactly the same moment, a great rumble began that sent the water trembling and wrinkling all about. Drops of cold water sprinkled down from the ceiling like the hints and starts of a rain shower.

Dantor ran down the ledge and hopped back into the boat. A stone lip erupted from under the water, creating a dam in the tunnel. A rushing roar reverberated from the darkness and the surface of the water grew agitated, rapidly lowering as if the boat was in a giant basin and the drain had been pulled. As the water receded deeper and deeper into a shaft, the elves gazed about themselves in awe. Torches on the dripping walls burst into flame, illuminating a striking kaleidoscope of reliefs in the stone. The collage told a tale of the dwarves and their mines: of their progress from pickaxe and chisel to drill and earthmover, of the discovery of gems and jewels without equal, and of the Great Mine Wars and the thousands slain in the cold dark depths of the mountains.

The water began to bubble and churn at the base of one wall until, at length, it receded below the ceiling of a tunnel which led away from the shaft. The dwarves waited until the water settled and torches on the walls were lit, illuminating the fully exposed tunnel. Then they pedaled and the vessel eased inside.

At the end of this tunnel was a dock, but this one had a wooden staircase with short, dwarf-sized steps leading up to a stone ledge. Above the ledge was darkness, but the echoes of drips and trickles of water could be heard.

Once the longboat was docked, two dwarves together grasped the handles on the sides of each of the large chests and lifted them out of the hull. Without a word, they worked together to place the chests on a wooden platform attached to a system of ropes and pulleys. With several of them grunting and pulling at the end of a rope and the squeaks of the pulleys echoing in what sounded like a vast space, the dwarves brought both of the chests to the top of the stone ledge. Then everyone mounted the staircase, where the dwarves lit torches that they carried to revealed a cavern of immense proportions.

It was apparent that it had been chiseled out of the rock to exacting dimensions, with straight walls and ceiling, but the trickle of water and mineral had, over the ages, formed a great forest of stalactites and stalagmites of a wondrous array of colors and shapes, all of them glistening in the light. The air was stagnant and musty as if it hadn't stirred in ages immemorial.

"These were our great mines of old," King Bufus

said as he led the way down a sparkling path of quartzite rocks between great columns of glittering stone. "But when gold was discovered in the wilderlands, the cost to mine the gold exceeded its value. That is why we no longer rely merely on mining. We are makers of machines—tinkerers, craftsmen, and inventors. So if, king of the Elves, ye ever find yer kingdom more prosperous than it is now, don't forget us. We can surely make something for ye."

"My kingdom," said Santa, "is not of this world. It should be among the stars."

"Well, my lad," King Bufus said grimly, "at the moment, yer kingdom is here, in the depths of the mountains." Then he raised his torch high and said, "Come! Come out! We have brought the star stones!"

From among the formations, one after another of the most pitiable assembly of thousands of elves appeared, each one gaunt and insipid and looking as if life itself was a heavy burden.

"They are refugees," Dantor explained, "hunted by men and by the Dark Elves of Balekhon. They had nowhere else to turn, so we provided them shelter. We store up starlight for them in crystals every night, but it is not enough. Their light is fading."

King Bufus said, "Beliach tightens the noose around our necks. Soon, we will be unable to protect them."

Myckel, his eyes expressing a newfound appreciation for their Dwarven hosts, said in something of astonishment and amazement, "You have done well. We are greatly in your debt."

"Indeed you are," King Bufus said, "And it is a debt that I hope you shall be able to repay, some day—provided yer king is worth his salt."

Santa said not a word, but walked towards a pair of elves who clung to one another, struggling to find their footing on the shimmering rocks. Their eyes were ghostly white and vacant.

King Bufus nodded towards them, "They won't last much longer. They lose their sight when draws near the end."

Santa compassionately covered the elves' eyes with his hands, to which one of them said, "Who touches me?"

"I am your light," Santa replied. When, having withdrawn his hand, the elves blinked, their eyes were clear and gray, and they looked about themselves in disbelief and awe. All the other elves who had witnessed this rushed like a wave towards Santa, saying, "Who is he?"

Kintel, overcome by excitement, capered into the fray, merrily shouting, "He is your king! He is the one foretold—the one to free you!"

The impoverished elves were touching Santa, and

he greeted them in turn, and the color returned to their faces, their eyes were brightened, and their vitality was restored.

Staring in amazement, Dantor said, "He really *is* the king of the elves."

King Bufus nodded to the chests, "I suppose we won't be needin' these starlight stones."

Myckel said, "We are on our way to Balekhon. He will destroy Beliach and free us from bondage."

Dryrie, for her part, stood motionless and stiff, with tears streaming down her cheeks. Myckel asked her, "Why do you cry?"

She bit her lip, then said, "I am grateful that what might have been was not."

Tenderly, Myckel asked, "*What* might have been?"

She shook her head, wiping her eyes. She said, "I believe now that he is the king."

"*Our* king," Myckel smiled.

When, having done all they could for the elven refugees, the company of elves parted ways with King Bufus, Dantor, and all the dwarves, they did so with well wishes. King Bufus warned them to be wary in the forest of Ashet, for Beliach's Dark Elves lurked there, searching for any Good Elves they might yet capture. He also told them that the kingdom of

Balekhon was ruled by a cruel and treacherous king—a man who would stop at nothing to deliver them to Beliach.

The Ashet forest was of towering trees with roots thickly weaving in and out like giant, tangled balls of yarn. For the elves, walking through this labyrinth of roots was a gloomy experience. Little sunshine made it through the lofty branches, there were no guideposts to show the way, and the roots never allowed them to see more than but a short distance ahead. Santa led, but gave no indication as to if or how he knew where he was going. What the other elves did not know and what Santa did not tell them is that they were being watched and followed.

After many days' travel with painful feet and dampened spirits, the companions began to doubt their leader. It seemed that they were seeing the same twists and turns of the roots over and over again. Myckel stopped and said, "We should have been to the Sea of Meteran by now. Are you sure you know where you are going, Santa?"

Not even turning to look at him, Santa said, "I do."

Myckel grunted in response, but continued to follow.

They were soon heartened by the sight of some sprigs of grass that cropped up here and there among the roots. These steadily increased until the trees cleared to reveal a green slope down to a beautiful, bubbling stream. Pleasantly situated against this was an appealing little cottage. Flower boxes ornamented the windows, and a trail of wispy smoke rose from a stone chimney. Attached to the dwelling was a wheel that collected the water from the stream and cheerfully splashed it into a gutter. A garden lined with tidy rows of the ripest, heartiest vegetables was confined by a fence of woven sticks.

"How beautiful!" Dryrie exclaimed.

"Who would choose to live in these terrible woods?" Myckel said.

"We shall soon see," Jaylit said, skipping down the hill.

"We must be cautious," Santa warned. "I wonder at how they make their living so far from any road."

"There's only one way to find out," Jaylit called back. Dryrie followed him, and Myckel said to Santa, "Perhaps whoever lives here can tell us how to get out of this forsaken forest."

Santa countered, "We are not lost."

"Your pride blinds you, my friend."

Santa said, "I will not go to that cottage. It is unwise."

Myckel corrected, "It would be unwise for us to continue in these woods without direction. Time is running short." With this, Myckel stomped down the hill, leaving Santa alone.

Jaylit knocked on the old wooden door. There was no response, and after a few moments he pushed it open. In the blink of an eye, several doves flew out, almost colliding with the elves' faces as they flapped for the sky.

The elves gingerly peered inside to find a pleasant-looking room with a hearth over which stewed a cast iron pot. There was a rustic table and stools, a large wicker basket, a sturdy chest, and some barrels. The table was a feast for the eyes, carpeted by a colorful spread of freshly cut herbs, carrots, potatoes, onions, squash, beets, bean sprouts, and all manner of the most appealing vegetables one could imagine. On the walls hung some knives, wooden spoons, and four wooden bowls. A delicious aroma of spices and herbs and every good thing wafted from the bubbling cauldron and richly filled the cottage. In a darkened corner was a stack of cages containing two squirrels, three rabbits, and ten chickens. The animals peeped at the elves through the wooden rods and, beginning with the chickens, struck up a chorus of noisy clucks, chirps, chitters, and screeches.

Jaylit plopped himself down upon one of the stools, "It would seem that fortune smiles on us. What a wonderful place to rest!"

“It smells so…delicious!” Dryrie said, curiously leaning over the pot.

“Delicious?” Myckel said in alarm. “But you know you cannot *eat.*”

“I know,” Dryrie said. “But I feel,” she touched a hand to her stomach, “*hungry.*”

Also reaching for his belly, Jaylit said, “If this is what hunger feels like, I don’t think I want to be hungry anymore.”

“Delicious!” came a garbled voice from the table. They all looked to see Kintel busily stuffing his cheeks with beets, purple juice soiling his little chin and fingers.

“Kintel!” Myckel shouted, rushing over to pull the beets from his hands, “This is not your food. *You are stealing*!”

Kintel sheepishly blinked up at him. He had not swallowed, so his cheeks were still full.

Myckel commanded, “Go outside and spit that out. You look like a fool.”

“Not to worry!” a pleasant sing-song voice came from the doorway. The animals immediately ceased their cacophony. “Keep him away from the vegetables, but he can have as much soup as he wants just as soon as I’m finished fixing it!” The voice came from a tall lady of magnificent beauty. The long, black tresses of her hair draped down her chest to her waist, and she wore a puffy white shirt under a tightly-strapped black bodice. Her skirt elegantly sashayed as she gracefully stepped into the room. “Whence have you come, my elven travelers?”

Chapter Eight

Baffled by her sudden appearance and embarrassed by Kintel's thievery, Myckel said, "I apologize for the intrusion. If you could just tell us the way out of this forest, we will be on ours."

"Oh, my, my. Lost, are you?" she fluttered her long eyelashes.

Jaylit volunteered, "We don't even know how lost we are."

Myckel cast him a warning glance, saying, "We simply need confirmation that we're on the right track."

"Of course," the lady said, sidling up to the table and extracting some parsnips from her basket. A rather large toad hopped out of her basket onto the table. As she laid the parsnips down, she said,

"Four darling elves,
four directions to travel.
Which way to go?
'Tis a myst'ry to unravel.
But first, some soup!"

"We are unable to eat," said Myckel. "We do not take food."

"Why ever not?" she demanded, rather harshly.

Jaylit said, "Because we're elves. Elves cannot

eat."

"Ah..." the lady said, "And elves live by the light of the stars. Is that what you think?"

"Yes," Myckel said. "Now, really we must be on our way." He nudged Kintel with his elbow.

"Oh, but you mustn't," the lady said, smiling agreeably. "Because I know that elves can eat just as any human can do."

Dryrie asked, "How do you know that?"

"Because," the lady said, pulling up her hair to reveal the loveliest pointed ears imaginable. "I, too, am an elf, and I eat as much as I wish."

Dryrie inquired with envious, wonder-filled eyes, "You eat?"

"And so too can you. Please, sit down. I should be so lonely to eat that whole pot of soup by myself."

Myckel forcefully protested, "We must be on our way."

But Jaylit and Dryrie, already perched upon the stools like eager children at their grandmother's house, agreed to try it. The elven lady leaned down to dab the juice off Kintel's chin, saying, "Your cheeks cannot hold those beets forever. You must swallow, my dear."

"Must I?" Kintel garbled through the beets. Then, squinting with concentration, he swallowed. At first, he stared with wide eyes as if he had been struck, but then this expression gave way to pleasure, and he smiled most blissfully.

"How is it?" Dryrie asked, leaning over the table towards him.

"You must try it," Kintel exclaimed, reaching for a carrot.

But the lady slapped his hand away, "No, no!" said she, her eyes darkened with irritation. "You must have the soup!"

Kintel coddled his pinkened hand.

She smiled demurely, "I'll fetch your bowls."

And so she did, filling each to the brim with steaming soup. Myckel said, "We must not eat! Do not listen to her!"

The lady smiled victoriously, "There isn't any harm in trying, is there?" She placed a bowl on the table before each elf except Myckel, who refused to be seated. She then directed, "Blow first, my darling little elves, or you could burn your darling little tongues."

Kintel did not have to be told twice. He greedily scooped a spoonful and impatiently huffed upon it before shoveling it into his mouth. After a satisfactory smack of his lips, he said nothing and fished for more.

Dryrie and Jaylit followed his example while Myckel watched on in dismay. "Stop it!" he said. "We must be going!" But the lady stared at him in triumph as his companions industriously satisfied the appetites that they had so suddenly received. Determined to seek Santa's help, Myckel turned for the door.

But it slammed shut in front of him. When he turned back around, he saw the elves leaning over the table with their chins in their hands, their eyelids drooping with drowsiness. The lady, who had before seemed so magnificent, was now hunched over, her silver, wiry hair topping her speckled, wrinkly face. The elven ears she had so proudly displayed were now replaced by ugly, bulging human ones.

Kintel dropped his spoon into his soup and fell facedown on the table, snoring. Jaylit and Dryrie followed.

With a much less pleasant voice, the woman eyed Myckel and said, "Your darling little elf-friends have all closed their darling little elf-eyes and fallen fast, fast asleep." With the steps of a cat, slowly and deliberately, she began to walk towards him. He reached for his sword, but much to his shock, his hand found an empty scabbard instead.

Making her way around the table and tapping Jaylit's and Dryrie's heads, she said, "Four darling little bowls for four darling little elves."

He backed away, feeling for the door handle behind him. When he grasped it, he found that it felt rough and cold. He spun around to see a boulder where the door once had been.

"One, two, three—but what's this? Only three have sipped their soup. Only three have slipped to sleep." With eyes and face reddened in fury, she glared at him, "One hasn't finished his supper!"

He valiantly dashed for the knife on the table, but as soon as he clasped it, before his very eyes it transformed into a sinewy stick. The haggard woman cackled as he tossed it down. He gripped a spoon, but that became a pebble. Piece by piece, the parts of the room vanished and were replaced by the murky woods.

There was no cottage, there was no stream, and there was no garden. He was standing in a ravine in the dark forest, and his three friends were sleeping on the ground. An enormous, boiling black cauldron stood over a glowing heap of hot coals. The only other thing that remained from the former scene was a pile of round cages with the animals stuffed inside, but now that he looked at them they appeared more miserable and less well-fed than they had formerly seemed.

Before he could chance an escape, wooden poles grew up out of the ground around him and twisted together at the top and the bottom, forming a much-too-small enclosure. A cage then sprouted around each of his sleeping companions.

The woman squealed, "One, two, three, four. Pity

that there weren't more! Oh well, these will do. Perfect pairings for my stew!" She hooted and laughed, holding her belly as she almost rolled onto the ground in delight. "Four darling little cages for four darling little elves!" She quizzically peered at them, "Now...which one shall I try first? The plumpiest, juiciest one?" She scratched her head and eyed Kintel with a lick of her lips, "Patience, Garbella. Save the best for last!" She pulled up her skirt and rushed over to Myckel's cage, hungrily eyeing him, "Or should I try the strong, fearless leader?" She threw her head up and cackled, exposing what remained of her rotted teeth.

I should perhaps take a respite from Garbella's dining conundrum to reacquaint you with Santa's part of the tale. He, unwilling to follow his friends to the cottage, had continued his track towards the Ashet mountains. He had hoped, I presume, that his companions would be quick to follow his lead.

Now, as I think I mentioned before, Beliach had circulated the notion that elves were not made to fly and were meant to stay on earth. The few elves whose shriveled wings had not entirely fallen off and who staunchly refused to remove them were forced to roam the wilds for fear of Beliach's Dark Elves.

One such elf was named Faybin, and although he

could not really recall flying, he refused to discount the notion that it was possible or that he had, in the past, done it. His wings were now not wings at all but ghastly protrusions of shreds and tatters. Rather than remove or alter them, he stubbornly insisted on allowing them to drag the ground behind his feet in the hopes that someday they might miraculously prove useful. So Faybin, having been banished from the company of elves, was now slipping in and out of shadows in the woods. His years of stealthy seclusion had rewarded him with a talent for spying (or otherwise sneaking and snooping about unnoticed), so it was no difficulty for him to follow Santa and his friends for mile after mile without their slightest awareness of his presence.

As Santa struck off alone, Faybin stayed behind, for he knew that the elves were falling into the clutches of an evil and despicable witch who could deceive even the shrewdest person through her powers of transformation. He watched them as they naïvely stepped into her counterfeit cottage. When the tall elven lady (whom he knew to be the witch) crept out of the shadowy woods and snuck to the door on the tips of her toes, her hands outstretched before her like hawk's feet and her long fingernails looking much like talons, Faybin became fraught with worry.

He stayed hidden there, wringing his hands.

Because he hated everyone, he saw no reason to interfere. The troubles of these elves were not his concern, he reasoned. And yet, he was overcome by discomfiting feelings that wouldn't leave him alone. The witch would eat them, he had no doubt, and being eaten is not a very pleasant way to die.

When the cottage suddenly vanished and all the elves were trapped in the cages, Faybin grew even more agitated.

But then, the witch suddenly shrieked, "Where is it? *Where is it!* Where is that blasted, old wand?" She looked to the toad that sat on her shoulder, "Did you see where I put it?"

In a peculiar, little voice her toad replied, "No, Garbella."

"Well it must be here somewhere! We've got to find it! You go that way and I'll go this way!"

The toad leaped to the ground and hopped off in Faybin's direction, saying, "Find the wand, got to find the wand!"

Garbella, on the other hand, was stomping off in the other direction, irritably shrieking and spitting and scratching her head.

Faybin jumped up some roots and into a branch, well out of sight as the toad passed beneath him. Then, when he could hear neither the witch nor the toad, he snuck down to the cages in the gulley.

Seeing him approach, Myckel demanded, “Who are you?”

“None of your concern,” Faybin replied, casually eyeing a pile of the elves’ weapons that Garbella had collected.

Myckel asked, “Do you know that witch?”

Faybin strolled up to the cage and said, “I know she’ll eat each and every one of you as soon as she can find her wand.”

“Please,” Myckel said, “help us.”

“And what will I receive in return?”

“Friendship.”

“I do not want any friends.”

“What do you want, then?”

Faybin eyed the weapons. “I could take anything of yours I want.”

Myckel impatiently demanded, “Are you going to help us or not?”

Faybin strode over to the weapons and picked out a sword. He found the scabbard that matched its ornamentation and buckled it around his waist. “A fine weapon. This sword, for your life.”

“And the lives of my companions,” Myckel said, nodding to the sleeping elves.

“I will free the animals,” Faybin said. He then proceeded saw open the squirrels’ cage.

“The animals?” Myckel exclaimed. Then, hearing

a shriek, he lowered his voice to a whisper, "But what of us?"

"There is more to these animals than meets the eye," Faybin said, prying open the cage and allowing the squirrels to happily scamper away. "I'll get to you if I can."

A hoot echoed from the woods, this time closer.

"She is coming back!" Myckel whispered. "She will be very angry if she sees you have set all her food free."

The rabbits were hopping off. Faybin now attended to the chickens.

"The chickens, too?" Myckel said. "Witch or not, the woman has to eat something!"

Only after the chickens had fled did Faybin turn to sever the poles of Myckel's cage.

But he was almost too late, for the witch's gleeful voice called out, "I found it! I found the wand!"

As soon as Myckel was free, he ran for another sword and set to work on the cages of his companions.

Garbella's voice came nearer and nearer, "Now, what shall I have with my soup? Not more chicken! I've had too much chicken already!"

Dryrie and Kintel were out of the cages and snoring on the ground. Myckel and Faybin worked together to free Jaylit.

"Rabbit? Too fleshy. Squirrel? Not fleshy enough. Duck? Too fattening. Pig? Too provincial. I want something special, something succulent, something refined."

Myckel and Faybin dragged Dryrie and Kintel into the woods and out of sight.

"I've got it! I know what I want. Some nice, tasty mutton. Or, even better, lamb! Four darling little lambs to fill Garbella's hungry little belly. Now all I need—" her voice abruptly stopped.

Jaylit was still lying by the cauldron, and Myckel was about to return from the shadows to rescue him, but Faybin stayed his shoulder. He whispered, "She is here. She will see you."

Garbella's voice suddenly came from the treetops high above the ravine, "What have we here? Four darling little elves—but three are missing!"

Jaylit suddenly began to move. His legs shrank, his hands turned to sticks, his face grew longer, and white hair sprung out over his body. Still sleeping, he rolled over. He now had four hooves, and his transformation from elf to lamb was complete.

The witch's voice came from a different corner of the ravine, "Where are you, my darling little elves? No need to hide!" Her voice traveled from one place to another as it said,

"Mutton, lamb, pork, or fowl?
Would you like to snort or howl?

It's your choice, what's your flavor?
Garbella has some soup to savor!"

She chuckled quite cheerfully. Myckel and Faybin looked towards the source of the voice, but could see no sign of her. Her voice came closer now, in the branches above them,

"No need to run or be afraid.
I'll season you nicely—before you're fileted."

But she wasn't there. The anxious elves started trying to pull the sleeping elves away, but then her voice came from right behind them. "There you are!" she hissed, "I found you!"

When they looked, they saw nothing, at first. But then they realized that the voice had come from a small spider. It held a tiny wand with one of its eight tiny legs.

Faybin leaped to crush her underfoot, but she scuttled to safety and taunted, "What a fool! You think you can squish me like a little bug? Squish me now, why don't you?" As she said this, she tapped herself with her wand and grew in size and form until she was a hulking, hairy mammoth. She held her wand in her trunk and swung her long tusks like two reaping scythes.

"Garbella the Gorgeous,
Garbella the Great!
You've met your match,
now meet your fate!"

She stomped towards them, stridently trumpeting. Backed against a tree trunk and with the tips of the tusks about to skewer him, Faybin volunteered, "If you please, ma'am! I want to be a goat!"

Garbella lowered her mighty tusks and, raising the wand out of his reach, rotated her wooly head to peer at him with a single eye. "What did you say?"

Fretfully, Faybin said, "I want to be a goat, if you please, ma'am!"

Scratching her hairy head with her wand, she said, "Goat? I've never had goat before. What makes you think I'd like it?"

"You said you wanted something special. What could be more special than goat? It's the preferred delicacy of kings and queens."

"Kings and queens?"

"But it is, ma'am. Goat has a wonderful texture—and the flavor is highly refined."

"Hmm," Garbella said. "I suppose you can be a goat if it is your last wish." And with that, she waved her wand and transformed Faybin into a mottled goat with a beard and stubby tail. He bleated.

"And as for the rest of you," Garbella squalled, "I don't care what you want to be! You're going to be what Garbella wants!" The tree leaned over and morphed into a single cage that contained all four of them, including the goat.

At this juncture, her toad returned and innocuously inquired, "Goat for your supper, Garbella?"

"Yes, I've heard it's quite refined," she said. "Now where is my salt?"

Myckel, now the only elf not asleep or transformed into an ungulate, said with his hands gripping the bars of the rooty cage, "Garbella the Great, you have surprised me. Lamb, goat, mammoth, and spider? Is that the best you can do? You are a hopeless witch if ever I saw one. The witch I knew in Simindra could make all kinds of things. Giant things, tiny things, and everything in between."

"Simindra?" Garbella said, grating some salt. "I don't know of a witch from Simindra."

"Prelanope the Profound, they call her. Could turn herself into amazing things, tremendous things, things you could only dream of."

"Could she, indeed?" Garbella said with a distinctly unenthusiastic voice.

"I suppose every witch is different. She must have

practiced a great deal more than you have."

"Practiced more than I have? Why—"

"It's understandable. You are so very busy with your cookery. Would you say you are more of a chef or a witch, really?"

Garbella, with many thunderous footfalls and puffs of dust, turned her significant mammoth bulk around. She frowned at him, "And I suppose you want me to demonstrate my witch powers by opening this cage?"

Myckel made sure to stand in the way so that she could not see the goat, who was industriously gnawing apart one of the shafts. "No," said Myckel. "But before you turn me to mutton or some such thing, might you show me just how large a creature you can become?"

"Look at me!" she cried, stomping her feet about and making quite a cloud of dust. "Isn't this large enough?"

"Well," Myckel said, "I am afraid not. Prelanopy could—"

From high in the treetops, a resounding voice thundered, "Prelanopy could what, my dear?" Standing before the cage where the mammoth had been, was a giant troll, its feet the size of boulders and its legs like the trunks of soaring cedar trees. It moved one of its feet, and the ground shook so violently that the sleeping elves and Jaylit the lamb were awakened. They gazed up in fright at Garbella the troll, whose face was so high that they could barely make it out among the highest branches.

"Quite impressive!" Myckel shouted. "I confess I never saw Prelanopy become anything that large. But what about something small? Can you become small?"

"I was a spider!" Garbella boomed, causing the trees to gently sway.

"Smaller than that, like a fly, perhaps? Just a harmless, little housefly?"

Garbella steadily shrank until she was the named diminutive insect, perched on a pebble. She shook her miniature wand at him as her voice piped, "What say you, now?"

"Well done! I don't think Prelanopy could—" Myckel praised, but he didn't finish because, in an instant, Garbella the fly was gone.

Her toad's tongue, unable to resist the fly that suddenly appeared before it, snapped out and captured her: wand, wings, and all. Having swallowed, the toad sat in stupefied silence for a moment, his bulging eyes appearing quite dazed. Then he screamed in a shrill voice, "What have I done? Garbella, are you in there?"

The goat finished nibbling the cage open, and Myckel emerged, paying little heed to the toad as he pried and prodded his fat toad belly, blubbering "Oh no! What have I done? Garbella? Garbella!"

Myckel made short work of freeing the rest of the elves (and the goat and the lamb), and having collected their weapons, evacuated the witch's ravine.

They tried to follow the direction Santa had been leading, and, at the fall of night, happened upon the elf himself. Santa wasn't surprised to see one elf missing from the party and the addition of two animals. He simply touched them on their heads and they were magically transformed back into their elven selves. Faybin, he praised for his quick thinking that allowed them to escape. To Jaylit, he said, "Next time, I should leave you as a sheep, for you were just as foolish as one."

Myckel said, "*I* was foolish, Santa. I am sorry I doubted you."

Chapter Nine

Wishing to put as much ground between the witch's ravine and themselves as possible, they continued their trek through the woods through the night, though Kintel, Dryrie, and Jaylit were hunched over with illness from the food they had eaten.

Faybin, finding himself uncharacteristically glad at the company of others, walked with them. Mile after mile he heard Kintel address Santa as "lord" and learned of Santa's past as mysterious newborn and future as magical king. This information, and the strange and wondrous implications of it all, began to churn inside him with more and more fervor until he could no longer suppress his need for absolution, so he finally leaped directly in front of Santa, and said, "If you are the elf king as they say, then tell me, what are these and what is their purpose?" Though intending to look intimidating, with a deep frown creasing his brow and his legs spread wide apart as if to prepare for a most momentous wrestling match, he made this demand rather pathetically, pointing a little finger to his bedraggled wings and appearing, on the whole, rather malnourished.

Santa frowned and brought a big hand up to stroke his beard. "Those are your wings. Why don't you fly with them?"

"I cannot. Look at them!"

"If the need arises and belief permits, you *will* fly."

"How can I believe when I see this?" he held up a tattered wing.

"You cannot fly because you do not believe me or what I say."

Faybin replied sharply, "What have you ever done for me that I should believe you?"

Santa replied, "All you must do is try."

Faybin gave Santa a suspicious look, then clenched his fists and appeared to be trying to make his wings move. But all they did was twitch.

Jaylit burst into merciless laughter, and Faybin's head fell. With shame, anger and dissolution, Faybin fled into the woods.

Faybin, you see, was so used to listening to the jeers of his fellow elves as they ridiculed his ratty wings, that he assumed Santa's intention through his words was no different. Thus he concluded that Santa was just as odious as everyone else, and he hated him.

The company persevered to the Sea of Meteran, the last obstacle between them and the kingdom of Balekhon.

The crossing of the sea gave the weary travelers not the reprieve they had hoped for, but instead held an adventure more terrible perhaps than all the others.

They began their journey in blissfully sunny weather, with but a light breeze to stir the water, but were soon dismayed to spy ominous storm clouds forming. A fierce wind began to whip up the ocean, and before long colossal waves the height of mountainous slopes were tossing the hapless elves up into the air as if they were little balls on a sheet that was being shaken by two delinquent youngsters. It was impossible to tell which direction the elves were going, or if indeed they were going any direction at all except up or down. Indeed, the waves were beating and bruising the elves so brutally, that they feared if it continued for much longer they should be too battered to survive.

A crest of one of the waves caught Myckel and pummeled him under the water. He was so waterlogged that he began to feel heavy and found, much to his surprise, that he was sinking. With another giant wave fast approaching, he cried, “Santa! Help me!” He was thrown into a deep and terrible fear, a dread of being overcome by the water, of slipping beneath the surface, and of never seeing light again. With the water enveloping Myckel's neck, Santa, the wind buffeting his white coat, called to him, “Myckel! Do not be afraid! Swim!”

But Myckel's head slipped beneath the sea, and he saw above him the undulating surface frothing and billowing, gray and ominous. Then he saw something else: Santa's hand reaching down for him. Santa gripped his arm and lifted him up.

When he was safely out of the water, Santa said, "Why did you not swim?"

"I did not think I could," Myckel said, shivering as the water dripped off his face. "I was afraid."

The elves continued their struggled against the sea until, as Kintel was flung high into the air by the frothing crest of a mountainous wave, he spotted the light of some flames in the distance. Where there was fire, there surely must be land, he thought.

As they passed one another in the air or met at the trough of a wave, he alerted the rest of the party, and, with great difficulty, they fought to claw towards this new target. As they neared it, they could see that it was a rocky island dominated by an intimidating stone fortress that perched on the cliff face of the coast like the mountaintop nest of a great and mighty eagle. A moat at the entrance to the stronghold was filled not with water, but with flames that licked up at the walls to a tremendous height and had charred the stone with heavy soot. There was no indication as to whose castle it was, for no banners ornamented its lofty towers.

As they stepped foot on the ground, they stared up at the ominous ramparts with unease. The hints of perhaps some long-past battle were found at the embrasures of the tops of the walls, where sharp markings had deeply scarred the stone. An ancient cobble path led up the hill, inviting the inquisitive to follow, and inquisitive they must have been (or very foolish) because they warily began to climb it. Sparse conifers clung to life from crevices in the rock, but the island otherwise seemed very much devoid of life. At points boulders blocked the way and the cobblestones were smooth, as if it had recently been a thoroughfare for water, no longer for hooves and wheels and feet.

They approached the gate and were surprised to see that the drawbridge was open over the fiery moat. Making a speedy crossing due to the searing steel on their feet and the blistering winds on their faces, they found themselves in a courtyard guarded by six soaring watchtowers, the tops of which were shrouded in the rolling black smoke from the flaming moat. A tall forebuilding with vacant windows ominously stood over the opposite side. Piled in great mounds along the sides and corners of the courtyard were jumbles of old ropes, rotting wooden frames, snapped poles, and torn fabric. Shards of pottery littered the cobblestone. There was total silence.

Santa walked to the nearest heap and pulled out a mass of tangled rope. He said, "These were ships." And indeed, it was true, for among the rubbish could be seen tackle, anchors, oars, and masts.

Santa led the way farther into the courtyard. As Dryrie walked, she thought she faintly heard the sound of a voice speaking her name. But the voice did not come from outside her head as if someone in the courtyard was saying it. Nay, it came from *inside* her. As she continued to listen for it, the voice grew in strength until it was as distinct as if she were speaking to herself.

"Dryrie," said the voice. "Dryrie, we know your secret. We know the burden you bear..." Dryrie felt a cold chill run from her head to her toes. It sounded as if the words were formed by a long, forked tongue. "Many years ago you made a wicked choice..." the voice hissed.

In her head, Dryrie said, "I know not of what you speak."

To Dryrie's horrific shock the voice responded, "Oh yessssss. We know. And we know more..."

"Leave my head!" said Dryrie in her mind, wishing she had some threat she could bring to bear against this voice.

"It would perhaps shock your companions if they knew of your ssssecret."

"I have no secret."

"In the dark of the woods...in the middle of night...something happened to you which has happened to no elf before. You bore a child, did you not?"

Dryrie shook her head.

"And this was an extraordinary child. You recognized that it was not fully elf, but also human. And you were deeply afraid. So you took your secret and you left him to die."

"*Not to die,*" Dryrie feebly said, a tear streaming down her cheek.

"You deceive yourself. You knew the winter cold would make short work of him."

By now Dryrie's face was dripping with tears.

"We think that your friends would be eager to know your ssssecret. It would be better for you if you did as we say."

"How do you know my secret?" Dryrie inquired.

"We are friends of Beliach. He knows all."

"He does not know *all.* Who are you?" Dryrie demanded.

"We keep our enemies close but our friends at a distance...."

The voice paused, waiting for her response, but she had none. She would not engage in riddle games with voices in her head.

"We are worth less than the ground we lie on...."

"I'm not playing with you," Dryrie said, feeling that she had gone quite mad.

"We have thousands of teeth that have no bite...."

Dryrie stopped walking. "*Dragons*," she said aloud. The other elves paused and looked at her quizzically. She nervously murmured, "Dragons are here!"

Chapter Ten

Myckel asked, "How do you know this?"

"They spoke to me—in my head."

"What did they say?"

"They," she hesitated, not wanting to divulge her secret, "they told me riddles."

"Riddles?" Myckel questioned.

Suddenly the pebbles on the cobblestones trembled as a powerful voice that seemed to echo from every wall thundered, "Yessssss, riddles."

The companions hastily formed a defensive circle, fearfully looking in all directions for the source of the voice.

The voice bellowed, "Licks, but never tastes. Eats, but never chews. Drinks, but dies."

Santa said low, "Fire."

The voice, now from one direction, said, "Exccccelent." Two bright orange lights, like two burning coals, shone from within the smoke shrouding the tallest tower. The smoke suddenly swirled away, revealing an enormous red dragon beating its broad, mighty wings. It clung to the tower, its huge talons neatly fitting into etches in the stone where they had clearly been innumerable times before. Its head bore two long, curving horns, its mouth was arrayed with symmetrical teeth, its neck was serpentine, and its long, winding tail ended in a spade shaped club. The smoke quickly cleared from the other towers, revealing five more dragons.

Santa shouted, “Run!” and led the way towards a doorway in the forebuilding. Jaylit, perhaps overcome by his fear (or, less innocuously, suspecting he had nothing to fear) stood in place like a stony statue. Apparently much to Jaylit’s surprise, Santa turned round to seize him by his collar and convey him to the doorway, closely followed by a billowing blast of scorching flames.

Inside, the party found themselves engulfed in darkness to which their eyes had no small amount of difficulty acclimating. Through the doorway, they could see the large legs of one of the dragons lighting in the center of the courtyard, its muscles quivering as it stepped towards the forebuilding. Dust and pebbles showered from the ceiling, and the dragon’s enormous, glowing eye peered inside. The elves dashed for the opening of a stairway that spiraled down into the ground. It was a short staircase, and in their haste they nearly toppled into a heap. At the bottom, they found themselves in a large passage that was nicely illuminated by the flare of an inferno that the dragon courteously blew after them. The ground shook with the tumult of huge dragon talons clawing away at the stone above.

Santa shouted a single word (that no one could make out) just before large stones from the collapsing ceiling rolled down the stairs and blocked the way, engulfing them in complete and utter darkness.

Dryrie lit her torch which, in such a deep and stagnant darkness, provided only enough light for them to find their footing on the scraggly rocks.

"Now what shall we do?" Jaylit asked.

"We cannot go back up," Santa said, "so we shall do the sensible thing, indeed, the only thing we can do: we shall go deeper in."

They had no choice but to follow Santa as he led them, though the rest of the elves were nearly blind and marveled at how he was able to move as quickly as he did. They began to breathe more easily with time, growing to trust their leader as he charted a course deeper and deeper into the labyrinth. The sounds of their pursuers growling and digging faded away, replaced by the steady drip, drip of cold cave water.

Dryrie's spirits sank to hear the dragon's voice once more, "Dryrie? Are you ready to do as we say, or would you prefer us to divulge your secret?"

"Leave me alone!" she cried in her head.

"But we only want one little question answered, and you shall never hear from us again."

"What is it?" she snapped.

"An elven party from afar.
But one is different, one a star.
Whence they came and where they go,
Who can tell, or do they know?
What a strange and daring mission.
Why the haste? Mere superstition?
There's more to this than meets the eye,
do tell us why this do-or-die.
Please solve this riddle for us, dear.
We won't tell secrets-don't you fear."

Dryrie cupped her face in her hands. If she told the dragons that they were going to the deep of Balekhon, surely they would warn Beliach! She said, "I won't tell you anything."

"We shall share your secret."

Suddenly Kintel said, "What is it, Dryrie?"

Startled, Dryrie said, "I said nothing."

"But I heard you say you have something to tell me."

Dryrie said sharply, "I said nothing!"

Myckel said, "I, too, heard your voice, Dryrie."

Dryrie stated, "I do not know what you heard, but it was not I!"

Firmly, Myckel said, "You told us you have something important to tell us."

"You are mistaken!"

"I heard you, too," Jaylit said.

In her head, Dryrie heard the nasty dragon voice, "Time is up. Tell us...are you going to Balekhon?"

Dryrie shouted in her head, "Yes!"

"Why? Who leads you?"

"Santa leads us. He is the one who was foretold, the king of the elves! He will fight Beliach and cast him into the deep of Balekhon!" As soon as she said this, she was filled with a deep and terrible dread.

"You have done well to tell us. If you make it there, you will see us at Balekhon."

Dryrie was deeply ashamed. Now, even if they found a way out of this dark cavern, she knew there was little chance they could fight the dragons who would be waiting for them. Her secret was safe, but the quest was now in serious jeopardy. She was doubtful Santa could fight Beliach, but to fight six dragons as well? Certainly, this was impossible. She was grateful for the darkness, that her companions could not see the tears that streamed down her cheeks.

For what seemed like days and days they walked in the darkness of the interminable cavern with not even a single speck of light to warm their spirits or guide them towards a route of escape. Despite this, remarkably the elves did not lose their health as would have been expected given the lack of starlight. They did, however, lose most of their spirits and perhaps some of their sanity with nothing to see but black rock and nothing to hear but the ceaseless drip, drip, drip of the trickling water.

Santa, it seemed, knew where he was going, and led them farther and farther along. Finally, when they thought they could go no more, they heard another sound.

Soft and gentle, piercing the impenetrable darkness with profound loveliness and grace, were youthful female voices. They sang in faultless harmony, their words inscrutable and yet alluring, their melody haunting and yet beautiful.

Then, out of the black void came a spot of light—like an oasis in a desert. Colors of lavender and turquoise and crimson shimmered and danced on the ceiling of the cavern, a spellbinding display in the dark. Like moths to a flame, the elves were drawn to it and soon realized that its source was an iridescent pool nestled in a fissure of sheer, smooth, walls. As they drew near it, the song became more insistent and more intense, drawing them into irresistible euphoria, as if they were in a trance. They leaned over the edge of the cleft and gazed into the glistening, crystal pool. There, reflected underneath his face, each elf saw an image of himself as he rushed down the steps to escape the billowing dragon flames.

At this moment, Santa raised his head and warned, "Watch no longer!"

But the elves heeded him not because they heard him not, so mesmerized were they. The images changed, now displaying each elf as he walked through the cavern. Again, the vision changed, now showing the silhouettes of the elves as they gazed up at the dancing lights from the pool. The images followed them from behind as they stepped up to the pool. And finally, they saw themselves hunched over the pool, looking down into its surface. And, reflected on the surface, they saw behind them faces with glinting eyes and mouths opening to reveal sharp teeth. The song terminated in a terrible chorus of shrieking, and the elves found themselves falling into the pool, shoved from behind by their unseen watchers.

The elves splashed into the cold water and, as soon as they righted themselves, looked up to see who or what had pushed them. But nothing was to be seen but the ceiling of the cavern, the light now flickering wildly with the agitation of the pool surface they caused. The shrieking had ceased, now replaced by echoes of their own splashes and coughs. And splashing they were, because this water was enchanted. They were unable to stand upon it as they normally would, but struggled to stay afloat. Desperately, they slapped the black wall of the fissure, but found it to be so smooth and so steep that it was impossible to gain a handhold.

For some time, they continued to thrash and splash, panic having set in at the realization of their plight. But, at length, their energy waned and they were still, moving only enough to stay afloat, which took considerable effort since they had never learned to swim before. And that is when several crystalline figures with long legs, long arms, and narrow waists stepped to the edge of the cleft and stared down at the helpless elves. They had glassy, blue skin, and their eyes were large and round and feminine and beautiful. Their lips parted as they eagerly licked them, their tongues long and curling and their teeth razorlike and brilliantly white.

"Who are you?" Myckel demanded.

One of the figures answered, her voice dancing off her tongue like chimes in a soft breeze, "We are nymphs of the underground waters."

Kintel, quite frightened, politely inquired, "What are you going to do to us?"

"We will wait," the first nymph said softly. "We have patience."

"Wait for what?" Kintel said.

Jaylit said with annoyance, "Wait for us to drown

so they can eat us, of course!"

Hoping to improve matters, Kintel said, "We are not very tasty, I am afraid!"

"Oh, but you are, or soon shall be," she said, and she eagerly caressed her lips with her tongue.

"Pray," Kintel said, "once we're dead, how will you fish us out of the pool?"

Her eyes flashed and she said, "Your questions probe too deeply."

"Please forgive me! I am a little impudent, I know. But I mean do you jump in after us? But if you did that, I should think you would have just as hard a time getting out as we would."

The nymphs laughed from above them, a delightful ring in a condescending sort of way. The first said, "You know nothing."

"What?" Kintel nervously asked, "What do I not know?"

The nymphs did not answer, but watched keenly, their eyes widening as they saw that the elves were having more difficulty staying afloat, their pointed chins bobbing in and out of the water.

Kintel was beginning to panic as his strength waned and the water crept up to his mouth. He knew he didn't have much time left.

The other elves were aghast as Kintel disappeared under the surface. Myckel cried his name and tried to rescue him from the water. But Kintel sank so fast that Myckel was unable to catch him. He dove in and saw Kintel rapidly sinking towards the bottom. But he wasn't, in fact, *sinking!* He was sweeping his arms out in wide strokes and furiously kicking his legs. He was *swimming.*

When Myckel did not return to the surface, the other elves also dove under and saw that both Kintel and Myckel were slipping through a crack near the base of the pool. They all swam through it and found themselves in black water which, once they kicked to the surface, they found to be in a different pool in a different room of the cave. There were no steep walls here, and they easily stepped onto dry rocks.

Chapter Eleven

Santa and the elves dashed for a passageway and, with as much haste as they could muster, put as much distance as they could between themselves and the nymphs.

Once they were certain the nymphs had not pursued them, Dryrie lit her torch and the elves continued to follow Santa through the dark tunnels and chambers. Weary of the endless travel in darkness, Jaylit said, “We escaped the nymphs, but I fear we shall yet perish in these caves. Is there no end to these tunnels and passages?”

“Quiet!” Santa warned in a whisper, holding up his hand. They listened quite intently for some time without hearing anything and just when some of them were beginning to lose patience, their hearts seemed to stop at the sounds that reached their ears. Hisses and whispers and syllables that could very well had been the chatter of serpents—should serpents be articulate. It was, without doubt, the product of breaths and tongues, calls and replies and banterings back and forth and over one another like a flock of reptilian birds.

“What are they?” Jaylit whispered.

Santa put a finger to his lips. But it was too late, for the sounds had ceased, replaced by a silence of the most apprehensive kind. Then, with eyes like black orbs protruding from the scaly top of its flat skull, a black head slid down from a crevice in the ceiling some distance away, and a blue forked tongue tasted the air. Its mouth opened, revealing a formidable arsenal of jagged teeth, and it whispered with the same hiss they had heard before. Several other heads soon joined it, leering down from other cracks. The first creature slid fully from the gap, exposing a very long and narrow body with four long and narrow legs, looking almost like a viper with appendages. Its feet ended in six spindly, ugly fingers with curved claws that easily clung to the rock.

"Psylodonts," Myckel said. "Take care that they do not touch you. They have venom in their claws."

The first psylodont effortlessly slithered along the ceiling towards them, pausing at intervals to taste the air. Its eyes, never blinking, were always upon them. Dryrie handed her torch to Myckel and nocked an arrow, but he said, "Their scales are too tough. You won't be able to wound it."

She ignored him and fired, but the psylodont moved not an inch and watched quite nonchalantly as the projectile ricocheted off its back.

Santa said, "Let us go!" And the elves followed him as he rushed ahead through the cavern. One by one, more psylodonts slipped from cracks and crannies all over the ceiling, their claws making little clacking noises as they slinked over the stone with ever greater assurance and speed as their numbers multiplied. The creatures easily kept pace with the company and Santa quickened until, with the passage narrowing, he was running at the limit of his strength. With the rock walls closing in around them, the elves had to duck to evade the claws of the psylodonts as they took lazily clumsy swipes at them. It was as if the psylodonts were so certain of the inevitability of the capture of their prey that they saw little need to put very much effort into it. But, quite suddenly, the ground gave way beneath them and the elves found themselves tumbling down a long, narrow chute where, at the bottom, they landed in a pile.

They were in a colossal chamber illuminated by firelight and filled with the din of roaring water, shouts and groans, cracks and clatters, footfalls and splashes, and all manner of noise. They could not see the source of any of this din, however, for they were behind a long heap of stones. With a watchful eye on the opening of the chute to be certain no psylodonts were in pursuit, the companions climbed up the stones and peeped over the top.

Immediately before them was a great river of ruddy water that steamed as it bubbled over rocks. Beyond this was a mountainous hillside of rock with a trail of torches leading up to the top where slope met ceiling and an opening like a giant keyhole was the entrance point for a steady stream of children wearing little loincloths and bearing upon their bent backs yokes stringed with big barrels. The children were shouted at and whipped mercilessly by the most hideous assortment of pale goblins one could imagine. The goblins had bulging, sallow eyes and pointed ears tucked neatly under pointed caps, gangling arms and legs, potbellies, and extremely long, yellow fingernails which they had fastidiously filed to fine points. It appeared that they fancied themselves quite handsome, for they had adorned themselves lavishly with jewelry of all shades of red and orange: garnet rings, topaz necklaces, citrine amulets, and copious earrings with giant rubies. Their gurgled voices sneered and sniveled as they berated the poor children, and their whips, constructed of woven black cords, left the little one's legs pink.

The children formed a steady chain from the top of the hill to the water's edge where they filled their buckets and back to the entrance. They stumbled under the weight of the sloshing buckets.

Santa said, "This is what becomes of children kidnapped by the Dark Elves."

"This, and worse," Myckel said. "We have reached Balekhon, the domain of the vilest of men."

"And of goblins," Dryrie said with disgust, nodding towards two of them that were bickering on the shore over some jewelry.

"Do not let them see your elven ears," Santa said. "They will kill you without question. Now quick, be on your feet. This is the surest way to get where we're going."

"It is also the surest way to get hanged!" Myckel whispered.

Santa stood to his feet and jumped up to the top of the rocks.

In response to his abrupt appearance, the goblins withdrew their daggers and nocked their arrows. An especially decorated goblin shouted at them, his voice sounding as if it came through his rather diminutive nose, "Stop! You are in the domain of the King of Balekhon! You shall be arrested and forthwith be conveyed to answer for your many crimes!"

Santa shouted back, "What crimes?"

"Spying upon the king's men unawares!" the goblin sneered. "Invading the king's property! Being in possession of a generally suspicious nature!"

Santa leaped off the piles of rocks and splashed into the river, which was shallow. With long strides, he confidently crossed it. Myckel hesitated, and they watched as the goblins easily took him into custody, taking his axe. The goblin chieftain examined his axe and said, “This is not permitted. It has both a sharp edge and a blunting backside. What do you call it?”

“It is an axe,” Santa said.

“Methinks this axe is proof positive of the nefarious nature of your business. Have you any other weapons on your person?”

Santa shook his head.

“Any blades hidden away?”

“No,” Santa said.

“Anything in your shoes of which we should be aware?”

“No.”

“Have you ever been convicted of any crime?”

“No.”

“And what is it you were doing by the king’s secret spring?”

“Looking upon the water.”

The goblin nodded knowingly to one of his companions, “Add that to his list of charges! Thievering the king’s water!”

“I said I was looking upon it.”

“We ‘eard you! And next you’d be stealing it, sure as my precious jewels! Now, enough prattle! Time to put you before the magistrate!” With a sly smile, he said, “Since you’ll be going to the city, you might as well carry these barrels.” He tapped four empty barrels that stood nearby. “Hopefully you have more strength than the scrawny little vermin that brought these here. Fill them with water and it's up the hill with you!" The goblin pushed the barrels over and commanded, "Fill them up and away we go!"

Santa dragged the barrels down to the shore and filled them with water. Then he took first one yoke and then the second so that all four barrels hung from his back. He leaned forward as he bore the weight.

With a snort, the goblin chieftain pushed Santa up to the base of the hill, the murky water sloshing up to the rims of his barrels. The goblin shouted to all the children who had stopped to stare at the spectacle, "Back to work, you putrescent, ugly little vermin!"

As Santa began an arduous climb up the hill, Myckel was overcome by rage at the injustice of it, and, followed by the others, he leaped down from the rocks and splashed across the river, sword raised. The goblins reacted swiftly, drawing their daggers and aiming their black bows and arrows.

With a voice strong and echoing in the cavern, Santa said, "Put away your swords! This is the only way!"

The elves reluctantly complied. The goblins, chuckling to one another in great delight at the ease and rate at which they were procuring prisoners, took their weapons and tied their wrists.

So it was that the elves were pushed up the hill by a throng of sniping, snorting goblins. At the top, they entered a crude tunnel which was clouded by acrid, black smoke from the many torches that the goblins carried. They shared this tunnel with the innumerable bedraggled children slogging along in both directions. The children took an interest in Santa with his white coat and white hat—the one his tawdle mother had so lovingly crafted all that time ago. Santa gazed upon each of their hopeless faces with the deepest of pity—bound and bullied though he was himself by the goblins.

After a long trek through passages that wound and coiled with seemingly no aim nor end, they suddenly stepped up a flight of stairs and through a jagged opening onto a thin ledge on the face of a cliff. A gray sky thick with menacing clouds that angrily roiled and churned overhead provided little light on their surroundings, but many flights of rocky steps led down to the base of the cliff where the poor children struggled with their barrels over a pile of rocky debris and into a thick forest, goblins with torches along the way hounding them for more speed and less spillage. The elves were driven along, quite regretful that the sky was so overcast and they were unable to catch even a passing glimpse of the stars before entering the thick woods.

The path snaked through the damp forest over ridges where rocks jutted out from the ground and down valleys where streams trickled over polished stones. The goblin's torches flickered and crackled, casting wiry, black shadows and discharging thick, black smoke that rose through the scraggly branches of the trees where perched vultures that eagerly leered down at the children.

Aside from the vultures, no animal was to be seen, and the smoke grew denser as they proceeded until they came upon a roaring wall of flame that was swallowing up the forest and everything in it. Goblins and men, with much bickering and uproar, were overseeing the fire. Beyond the flames, the ground was being flattened and a great road was being laid down one brick at a time by countless laborers: men, women, and children, each of their faces grim and blotched with soot. Here, goblins were not the only enforcers of industry, but soldiers in flashing silver armor astride black horses galloped up and down the ranks, thrashing their sabers and mercilessly shouting through their helmets.

The line of children streamed down the road, joined by a steady traffic of men and mules weighed down by cargos of bricks. The road led straight through the forest, fallen trees still smoldering on both sides, until it passed through a bulwark of dirt, logs, and bricks. Inside, the elves found that the road was crowded with scores of goblins and humankind traversing every which way. All the goblins were wearing flamboyant jewelry and all had an air of superiority about them with their wart-covered noses held high and their eyebrows lifting with disdain as they looked upon the humankind about them. Many goblins were dressed in puffy pants with sashes crossing their chests, and many rode astride large, two-legged, muscular beasts with long snouts full of jagged teeth, piercing eyes, and colorful crests on their heads that rose when they snarled. The beasts were quick, darting in and out of the rabble with ease and making chirruping sounds.

The humankind, for their part, were of a motley assortment and were, with few exceptions, burdened by heavy cargo—baskets, barrels, pottery, and bricks. They ranged in age from the very young to the mature, but there were no old among them.

The descending, winding road was edged by rudimentary mudbrick structures that were fortified with straw, wooden beams, and sticks. Draped over doorways were coarsely woven banners of subdued, dark colors: ochre, ivory, crimson, black, and indigo. Narrow alleys intersected the street.

The goblin captors pushed the elves down the street, shouting, “Make way for the king’s prisoners!”

This incited the goblins they passed not only to make way, but also to spit upon the elves and to utter curses.

Myckel said under his breath to Santa, “We are here to fight Beliach. Our capture is a futile distraction. Has your loyalty to men blinded you to the cause of the elves?”

Santa said, “It is the blind who need me. To them I am loyal.”

“Stop your jabberin’!” the lead goblin shouted, striking Santa across his legs.

Upon rounding a bend in the street, a view of a market was presented, with fat, hive-shaped woven huts and crude bowers that protected wares for sale. Here, goblins were engaged in a shouting match as they proffered all manner of merchandise, from spices and legumes and livestock to pottery and textiles and jewels.

Beyond this were more mudbrick structures which increased in size and height until imposing gray stone buildings replaced them, these forming the veritable foothills of a soaring brick mountain—an auburn tower with doors and windows opening to a circling path that coiled its way around and around higher and higher until it reached the top, where perched an ornate, black citadel. The storm clouds in the sky circled above the city in a wide spiral, dark and churning. Lightening flashed and cracked above the citadel, its thunder rolling down from the tower like crashing waves over an enormous beach.

On the side of the marketplace was a large classically-styled building coated in a layer of white plaster that had stripped away in places, revealing the mud bricks underneath. Several skewed, cracked columns supported a roof that had been, at one time, etched with designs of the kind seen on the goblin fabrics, but was now crumbling with age. The goblins pushed their prized elven prisoners under the vestibule and through a pair of heavy wooden doors that sagged on their hinges.

Once inside, a weary Santa cast off the yokes and dropped the barrels to the floor. They were in a hall with wood-paneled walls that, though at one time were doubtless polished and fine, were now grimy and pocked. Marble busts of eminent goblin magistrates sat on top of small columns against the walls. Ornate candelabras held candles both lit and extinguished, and piles of wax had built up from the floor beneath them like stalagmites in a cave. The ceiling was whitewashed plaster, with bits and pieces of it having fallen away where water dripped, revealing moldy stone underneath. A great stained glass window overlooked the hall from the far side. It was dark and inscrutable until the flashes of lightning outside illuminated the image of a goblin reaching up to touch the hand of a man wearing a crown. Below this, on a high wooden platform behind a tall wooden balustrade, on a little brass stool sat a plump goblin fast asleep. His warty face was rather severe, even in slumber, and he wore a black robe that was so much too big for him that folds of it were heaped upon the floor around his stool. A white wig graced his crown, the curls of which were parted around his especially broad, pointed ears. He wore no jewelry save for a single ring with a big, black diamond. He was leaning back against the wood-paneled wall and snoring shrilly through his miniature nostrils. To his left sat a very small goblin at a writing desk. He held a large feather in his hand. A goblin dressed as a butler stood in a corner near a table with a decanter, and several goblins in armor stood at attention at the front and back of the hall.

The goblin chieftain cleared his throat and, in a strident voice, shouted, "Your worship, Magistrate Ruthorspat!" As soon as this was said, the small goblin began to scribble furiously, the feather flitting about at such a pace it appeared it could have flown away.

The magistrate's bulging eyes fluttered open and his stool tipped precariously before he righted himself, his head twitching back and forth as he sleepily took in his surroundings. He groggily blustered, "Who comes before the king's court this day and for what inauspicious purpose?" A piece of the ceiling suddenly dropped down and landed before him with a crash, but he seemed to take no notice of it for there were pieces of the ceiling all about the floor.

Chapter Twelve

The goblin chieftain sniveled, “We have apprehended these criminal vagrants, your worship, for wielding lethal as well as very unsafe weapons, for thievering the king’s water, for being in possession of a generally suspicious nature, for invading the king’s property, and—” the goblin frowned. He snapped his fingers, “There were quite so many offenses methinks I’ve neglected to commit the last one to me memory.”

His absentmindedness seemed to matter little, however, for, while he had listed out the crimes he did recall, he had been rewarded by increasingly aghast expressions of disbelief as well as snorts of disapproval from the magistrate. Another of the goblins volunteered, “I know what it was, your worship! They was spying upon the king’s men—unawares!” he smiled, his pointy teeth exposed quite charmingly.

“Ah, yes of course. They was spying upon us without we having the slightest inclination that they was there!”

Magistrate Ruthorspat said, “This is a grave list of crimes, indeed. Is there no longer any respect for the crown among the human rabble?”

The goblin chieftain bowed, “’Tis a fleeting sentiment, indeed it is, your worship!”

"And what of the weapons? Let us have a look!"

The goblins brought forth the bows and swords, dropping them in a clattering heap before the magistrate, who reacted by biting his long, yellow fingernails. When the gobbling chieftain produced Santa's axe, however, pointing out with vivid demonstration that it had "both a sharp edge for slitting and a blunt backside for clobberin'," the magistrate nearly slid off his little stool. Collecting himself and resituating his wig, he exclaimed, "I have seen quite enough! Transport these villains directly to the his majesty King Karbondor with the utmost of haste!" And with that, he sounded his gavel a number of times and called for some wine to be brought immediately, wiping a sweat from his brow.

The small goblin finished his scribbling, dropped some wax from a candle onto the parchment, stamped it, and held it out over the edge of the balustrade. The goblin chieftain was quick to snatch it up and usher the prisoners outside.

The elves were conveyed through street after street of disordered goblin haunts and hordes which made up the outskirts of the city. At length, they came upon a broad cobbled street where majestic horses trod, some pulling wagons and others carrying men in glinting silver armor. Lining the road were flaming torches on tall stands.

The road crossed a magnificent stone bridge with lancet arches over a chasm. At its base was the deep Ufratin River, its gray water rushing so speedily around the bend that it veered up the wall. On the other side loomed a formidable wall of cut stones—each the size of a boulder. Once they crossed the bridge, they were confronted by a sentry at the thick, iron gate.

The goblin chieftain rang out, "These are prisoners of the crown! His worship Magistrate Ruthorspat has demanded that they be hastily conveyed directly to his majesty King Karbondor!" He presented the parchment with much flamboyance.

The sentry quickly skimmed the parchment and nodded, ushering the elves through the gate but stopping the goblins, "The king's guard will escort the prisoners from here."

The goblin chieftain protested, "But it was us who caught them!"

"As you are well aware, goblins are welcome to conduct the king's business, but they are not welcome in the king's court!"

The goblin chieftain exposed his sharp teeth and bowed, batting his eyes as he said, "Perhaps an exception might be made this once due to our extraordinary service and loyalty to his majesty?"

In response, the sentry gave the order, and the gate was closed with a clattering crash.

The streets were paved with gray stones, each one snugly fitting against its neighbor so that the elves' feet could scarcely tell one stone from the next, so smooth was the surface. A gutter on the side of the street carried a constant flow of water. The buildings, also constructed of gray stone, were, at the least, ten floors tall and engraved most meticulously. Many of the gables were leafed with gold, as were the ridges in the shafts of the many columns that decorated the doorways and windows. In great contrast to the many streets they had traveled before, these were nearly vacant, save for soldiers on horseback and the line of children who bore the barrels upon their backs.

The soldiers in silver armor escorted the elves up a steeply inclined thoroughfare which terminated at the base of the enormous tower that rose up into the air like the face of a cliff. Banners that fluttered in the strong wind at the top were mere specks in the elves' sight, so great was the height. Circling around and above the tower silently, their shadows streaking across its brick surface, were six red dragons.

As they made their way up the street, people emerged from buildings to gawk and to jeer. They were dressed quite resplendently in black and white laced with silver, and their faces were powdered white.

Upon their heads were white wigs with curls as round as pearls or locks as straight as swords. They wore silver jewelry with diamonds that glittered in the flashes of lightening.

They came to a wide plaza surrounded by extravagant buildings. Steaming water flowed down trenches from a bathhouse at the far side. The entrance to the bathhouse was edged by two columns and at their bases sat two men behind two marble tables. They wore crowns and were counting piles of coins. As people entered the bathhouse, they placed coins upon the tables. A polished statue on an enormous pedestal occupied the center of the courtyard. Portraying a man raising a sword as he sat atop a rearing stallion, it was tall and magnificent and was briefly bowed to by the people who passed it. The figure wore a flowing robe and pointed crown, and his eyes, though made of stone, were fierce and full of wrath. On the pedestal were words etched in the human tongue: HIS MAJESTY KING KARBONDOR THE GREATEST AND HIGHEST AND MOST POWERFUL. White flowers and other tokens of adoration had been laid at the statue's foot.

Kintel whispered to Santa, "He must be a great king; indeed, the people love him so."

Santa cast off the barrels and said, "Men worship power, in all its forms. He is a great king, but he is not a good king."

One of the soldiers leaped off his horse. Swinging his blade to stop just at Santa's neck, he snarled, "What did you say?"

"I said that Karbondor is not a good king."

In a rage, the soldier knocked the white cap off Santa's head. When the people in the plaza saw his elven ears emerge, a great cry of shock and horror rose up from them.

The soldier shouted, "He is an elf!" To the people, the soldier shouted, "Elves are not to exist! It was they who slaughtered your children!"

The people all rushed around him in a great mob, screaming curses at him and spitting at him, their angry eyes widening on their skeletal white faces.

"What shall we do with this elf?" the soldier roared.

The people screamed in fury, "Kill him! Let him die!" They began to beat him most mercilessly and some drew their knives as if to carve his elven ears from his head.

The soldier jeered, "Are you an elf?"

"I am," Santa said, though his condition was so pitiable. "I am the king of the elves."

With this, a horrible laughter grew in the mob, and the soldier placed his white cap back on and bowed as if in reverence, crying, "Oh mighty king of the elves!"

Then, with the crowd growing ever more agitated

as if they should kill him at once, the soldier shouted, “He shall go before King Karbondor!” To Santa, he spat, “Take up your water! We shall see the king of the elves bow before the king of all Euchaia!”

Santa, wincing at the pain as the yokes pressed onto his neck and shoulders, lifted the barrels of water once again.

Slowly, the soldier raised his sword and, in silence, remounted his steed.

The party continued their walk up the street until they reached the base of the tower. From this vantage point, the height to the top was truly dizzying. The road which spiraled up the tower was wide enough for perhaps six horses, and was made of small steps. The first line of children was here joined by three others and they all made their way up the road, the barrels still sloshing on their backs and armored soldiers still screaming at them for more haste.

Without a moment’s delay, the elves were pushed up the first steps. For Santa, every step was a terrible strain, but not a word did he utter nor did he make a sound. Somehow, he found his footing step after step. The soldiers, their faces hidden beneath their helmets as if to hide their identities from the cruelty they inflicted, forced the elves to walk closest to the perilous edge. As the height of the climb increased, so too did the wind, and it buffeted Santa and threatened nearly to hurl him off the staircase.

Whereupon they had come nearly halfway up the tower, they came upon a child with the weight of yoke and barrels upon him who stood at the edge of the stair looking out. His hair was whipped by the gale, with the ominous clouds swirling high above and the thunder rolling over the dark landscape of city and fiery woodland and raging sea below, and his eyes were still and distant. Some soldiers were striking him with their black whips, but he moved not nor seemed to have any awareness of their shouts and blows. And, indeed, the soldiers were somewhat restrained for the child's feet touched the very edge of the stair and one blow too brutal could send him tumbling down with his precious barrels.

Santa, lifting his head from under the heavy yokes, shouted, "Quiet! Leave the child alone!" The soldiers, surprised, ceased their cruelty. Then Santa did something which amazed and awed his companions. He fought to climb the steps up to the child and placed a trembling hand on his back, saying, "Be of good cheer, child! Come, let me take your burden." And Santa, the king of the elves, knelt with his head low, and took the yoke from the child. Now, heavy-laden and weary with all the barrels upon him, he let forth a great cry and lifted himself to his feet, his legs quaking beneath him.

The child slowly turned and, blinking in the wind, gazed upon Santa as if his eyes were beholding the first kindness they had ever seen and as if his heart was brimming with the first rays of hope it had ever felt.

The soldiers, out of some deep cruelty that dared not allow them to take pity on either the child or Santa, began to strike him and mock him, quite amused by the fact that he was already overburdened with two yokes and now chose to take on a third. The child was left to slink away down the steps—once he came to his senses.

As the march up the stairs became too difficult and Santa stumbled, Myckel and Kintel came to his aid and held up his arms on either side.

Having reached a height such that the churning clouds above seemed close enough that their coils and tails might lick down and touch them, the elves were alarmed that the dragons whooshed by them quite closely, their long bodies carried by their broad wings which blew great gusts of air that threatened to knock the elves off their feet.

Suddenly, one of the foul beasts lighted right before them, with the children and soldiers fleeing up and down the stairs to make room. The dragon's serpentine neck curled around to hover just above the company of elves. With eyes burning red and a voice booming and guttural, the dragon said, "You'll excuse my interruption. But I wanted to pay my respects to the king of the elves—before his execution."

Myckel angrily retorted, "How did you know we were here?"

"You can thank your friend Dryrie for that."

The companions all looked at Dryrie, their faces aghast and questioning.

Dryrie exclaimed, "I do not know of what he speaks!"

The dragon's lips curled up in a smile: a wrathful, delightful smile that bared his uniformly daggerlike teeth to menacing effect. Another dragon landed behind them, beating its wings so powerfully that they were buffeted by a fierce blast of hot wind. The two beasts took turns in spitting out a riddle:

Sow and grow until they die,
feed and weed until they cry.
Start with one and make a lot.
All it takes is but a thought.
He who plants them is not wise.
What seeds are these?
They're little lies!

The first dragon's eyes blazed like hot coals as it spoke the incriminating line. Then, snaking its head to look directly down upon Dryrie, it said, "We keep our word, but we see you cannot be trusted, Dryrie. Now here is a riddle for you to guess." Its breath hot and searing, the dragon bellowed:

"Born in cold and left to die.
A small baby, hear him cry.

Loved him not, she did not care.
Tell the elves? She did not dare!

Who was he? What was his name?
We won't say; this is a game.

Lord of elves, their crown and king.
He's the one the prophets sing.

But lo, what's this? Is that the one?
Is this the boy? Is this your son?

He does not look like king or lord.
He brings no army nor a sword.

What wears he? A crown to rule?
Yoke and barrels like a mule!

What a shame. The end is near.

The game is up it would appear.

The elves are through. A dying race.
They have no king, they have no face.

Thanks to you their tale is done.
You gave them up, you chose who won.

This is your fault, you made your fate.
The guilt is yours, you bear the weight.

Tell them now, the truth you hold!
Or must we, and be so bold?"

Dryrie's face was awash with tears and she could not look at Santa—now knowing that he was the child she had left on the altar at Bannonith so many years ago.

Myckel looked upon her with disbelief and anguish. He asked, "Is it true? Are you the one who bore the child?"

She dropped her head low.

"And you left him on the altar!"

The dragon, wickedly smiling, said, "And now I will take you to the true king: the king of men, the king of elves, the king of all Euchaia!"

With that, the dragons flapped into the air and

swooped down to gather each of the elves in their giant talons like squirrels plucked from the trunk of a tree.

With the wind quickly drying her tears and the city below appearing small and distant, Dryrie was carried up to the lofty top of the tower where a polished marble surface of black and white made a stark contrast to the ruddy bricks of the structure underneath. The line of children terminated at a circle of tall stones in the center of which was a black hole. Each child, upon reaching this hole, dumped the water of the barrels in it before turning away.

Dryrie was dropped with the rest of the elves before the citadel, with its black buttresses and arches and spires. A great doorway was framed by a deep archivolt. The doors swung slowly open. The dragons blew a half circle of fire around the elves, hemming them in against the structure. Santa's barrels of water had spilled all over the floor when he was dropped, and he cast aside the yokes as he straightened and faced the doors. "Come," he said. "Let us meet this great king of Balekhon." And he stepped through the doorway.

Inside was a long hall with soaring walls that arched up to a line in the center above. Soldiers in silver armor and helmets stood stoically in two lines, forming an aisle up to a series of steps that mounted the pedestal of a great throne which was shrouded in darkness. There was no sound until a voice loud and clear and aloof echoed from the throne: "Come!"

The elves walked up the aisle between the soldiers, who turned their heads to watch them as they passed. When they reached the throne, they could see that it was made of polished black stone and was sat upon by a large figure with black robes and a glinting silver crown with sharp points.

The harsh voice spoke, strong and confident and clear as crystal, "I have been expecting you. Word reached me of your coming long ago. Is it true what they say? Do you really believe you are the king of the elves?"

"I am," Santa replied.

"The elves need no king because they have no future. They are no more."

"The elves," said Myckel, "will be great again. Santa will defeat Beliach and his forces of evil and you will see the elves rise as you have never seen them before."

"I see no elves," the king. "There are no elves here. You see," he rose, revealing his tremendous height, "we live as men and rule men." With these words, all the soldiers removed their helmets to reveal black eyes, dark amethyst faces, and ears that had been sheared at the top, ugly scars in place of the graceful elven points that had once been there. “We are the inheritors of Euchaia!” He raised a long, black sword.

“You hold the blade of Lyadeth! Beliach’s sword!” Jaylit exclaimed with excitement. “How did you come by it?”

“Beliach was my name before,” the great elf seethed. “I am known to men as Karbondor, King of all Euchaia!” As he said this, his eyes glowed hot like blue flame and he was wreathed in dark blue light.

“Who are you?”

Jaylit gingerly stepped forward, his legs quaking as he stared up at the being before him, and, quite awkwardly, he bowed low, “I am Jaylit, your humble servant. Your majesty, you are indeed the greatest and highest and most powerful!”

“Jaylit!” Myckel shouted. “No!”

Gaining confidence, Jaylit stood, “You are a fool, Myckel. Santa is no king.” He walked to Santa, and with a look of evil shadowing his face, he spit on him and flung the white cap off Santa’s head. “You will be destroyed with all the other elves who refuse to honor Beliach!” Then, to Beliach, he said, “Sire, you must be made aware! The dwarves have betrayed you. They harbor a great population of elves deep in the ancient mines of Ashet. The elves there honored this ‘Santa’ as their king. They must be destroyed.”

“Viardech!” said Beliach. “Take Jaylit and our

legions and the dragons to Ashet and kill every last dwarf. As for the elves, you know what to do."

"Yes, King Karbondor," the elf knight Viardech said. "It shall be done." He and Jaylit walked down the aisle of dark elven soldiers and out the doorway.

A rage flashed in the eyes of Myckel, who suddenly seized the sword of the nearest soldier and shouted, "So long I have desired to face you. So long I have wished to avenge the lifesong that you silenced, Beliach!"

"So long have you wished—*in vain!*" roared Beliach. He nodded and a large company of the Dark Elves rushed up to surround and restrain Myckel, taking the sword from him.

Powerless, Myckel cried out, "Help me, Santa! Call your elves! They will hear you!"

"Call your vast elven army, oh king of the elves!" mocked Beliach.

Santa lowered his head.

Beliach pressed the tip of his sword to just below Myckel's chin, and black flames began to lick around his neck. Beliach said, "I took pleasure in extinguishing Kelia's lifesong.... I allowed her to cry out your name in the deep, black void so that it would echo in your ears forever. I see you hear her still."

Myckel clenched his teeth and his face trembled with rage.

"Santa," Beliach said, "will you save your friend, oh king of the elves? Call your legions!"

Santa was silent.

"I say you are no elven king!" Beliach roared. "You are no elf at all!" He smiled with contempt, "After all, where are your elven ears?"

Chapter Thirteen

"Tomorrow," said Beliach, "the king of the elves will hang by his neck before all to see! Lock them away."

So the elves, with the exception of Jaylit, who was on his way with the dark elven legions towards the mountains of Ashet, were cast into a dark cell in the citadel. With a small barred window, the only light that came in were flashes from the lightning in the churning clouds above.

As they sat there on the cold stone, Myckel said to Santa, "You do not mean to fight him, do you? You will not cast him into the deep, will you?"

"The deep is below us. He has built this great tower over it and has the children pour water, thinking that he can prevent his demise by filling it up. But he need not have done so."

"What are we to do, then?" Myckel asked bitterly. "Why did you bring us all this way?"

Just then, a small scraping sound was heard which grew more and more distinct until the bars of the prison collapsed into the cell and the voice of Faybin was heard, "My friends, are you in there?"

Great was the joy as Faybin helped Myckel, Dryrie, Kintel, and Santa out of the cell and onto a brick ledge of the tower. They admired Faybin's wings, restored as they were to their former beauty.

Greater still was the joy as Faybin related how he had heard Santa's voice calling to him for help and remembered what Santa had said to him about his wings. He had, once more, tried to make his useless wings useful and found, to his elation, that he lifted into the air. Swift indeed was his flight across the woods and over the mountains and the sea to Balekhon, where Santa had told him to go.

When he finished telling his tale, he turned to Santa with his face downtrodden, "You are the king of the elves."

Placing a hand on Faybin's shoulder, Santa said, "Do you believe because your wings were restored? You will see greater things than this."

Myckel said, "Hurry! We haven't much time! Beliach's forces are on the way to Ashet." He pointed to the red dragons that flew in the distance and the glints of silver armor that came from a vast army that was on the march down the road out of the city. "They will leave none alive."

Together, all the elves rushed across the stony top of the tower. But as they passed the circle of stones where the children were dumping their buckets of water, Santa stopped. He slowly stepped towards the black opening.

Myckel and the other elves turned around when they realized Santa had stopped. The wind beat Myckel's dismayed face as he cried in a voice that sounded like the last breath of hope, "Santa, king! What are you doing?"

"I will not cast Beliach into the deep. It is I who must go."

"Why?"

"It is only I who can save the elves. If Beliach fell into the deep, he would be free to ravage mankind for one night and day every year. I cannot allow that."

"But you will be entombed in the deep!"

"To free the elves, my freedom must be forfeit."

"But you are our king! You must lead us to victory against Beliach!"

"A great king gives himself up for his people. This is the only way, Myckel!"

"Do not use my name," said Myckel. "I do not know you! You are not my king!" Myckel was unable to reconcile his belief of what Santa should be with what Santa was, and he turned his back on him, tears streaming down his cheeks.

Suddenly, a deep roar bellowed over courtyard. The stone surrounding the door of the citadel burst outwards and cascaded with a great tumult all over. Beliach's great and beautiful figure, wreathed in black and sapphire light, emerged. He bore his long, flaming black sword. Santa stood over the edge of the deep and stretched his arms out. Beliach hurled his sword at Santa, the blade singing through the air, but it slipped past its target and clanged on the stone.

Santa leaned forward as if to fall.

Dryrie reached out for him across the chasm and screamed, "Son!"

A faint smile appeared on Santa's bruised face and he said, "Do not be afraid. You have found favor with the Morning Star!" And with that, he slipped off the edge and into the deep, a streak of white and red like a shooting star that fell deeper and deeper until it could be seen no more. His hat, having fallen off his head, lay on the stone edge of the chasm.

The elves, for their part, stared at one another with the most disbelieving awe. For there, on their backs, flashes and orbs were shining and sparkling until wings of light were formed.

With tears in his eyes, Faybin turned his head to admire his new wings, and when he found that, with a mere thought, he could make them flutter, he jumped for joy and soared into the air.

Myckel and Kintel were first unable to trust what had happened, but soon found they were flying with Faybin.

Beliach, on the other hand, stared into the abyss for a long time. But, gradually, he began to look at the other elves with the deepest of loathing, for he had been given no wings.

Dryrie forlornly gazed into the chasm, blinking away a spring of tears.

But, suddenly, a figure lighted before her. It was Santa, now radiant with white light. In a voice that sounded distant and at the same time close, like roaring water, he said, "Do not let your heart be troubled. You were chosen. You were blessed among all elves. Be at peace."

With his words, her beautiful wings fluttered hopefully, and she smiled.

Santa turned to Myckel, who said, "How is this possible? I thought you were to be entombed in the deep?"

"I am free one day of the year. This was the day of my birth those many years ago."

"Forgive me for doubting you," Myckel said, bowing. "King of the Elves, and our liberator."

Kintel was quite overcome by tears of gladness and could say nothing, but he held out the special red-stained cap which has now become the trademark of Santa's head. Santa gratefully accepted it and placed it upon his head.

Beliach, seeing that Santa was alive, gave an angry shout and held out his arm. His sword sailed through the air and landed in his grasp. He dashed for Santa, his figure a streak of sapphire and amethyst, and the black flames of his sword trailing behind him.

Santa bellowed, "You cannot come against me with sword or spear! I am the Morning Star!" As he said this, a great flash of light erupted from him and his eyes were blazing white. Beliach was cast onto his back, the tip of his sword igniting into hot flames. These white flames traveled down the length of the sword and onto his hand. Beliach dropped the sword, but it was too late, and the flames licked up his arm and engulfed his entire figure until he was no more.

Santa then looked up to the sky, with the dark, roiling clouds, and a bright shaft of radiance shone from him into the center of the storm. Bit by bit, the clouds dissipated until blue sky appeared and the city was bathed in a cheerful glow.

The little children, still bearing yokes and barrels, blinked up at the sunshine with trepidation, as if they had never seen the light of day before.

"Depart, children!" said Santa. "You are free!" Then he turned his attention to the dragons that flew above the dark elven army that was marching down the road out of the city.

"Where is my army?" Santa said. And, at that moment, a great cloud of elves with their radiant wings came down from the sky above him. "Go!" he commanded. “Put an end to this violence!”

The dragons suddenly found themselves hurling towards the earth in balls of white flame like shooting stars and Santa’s elves soared down from the tower to attack the dark elven army.

Myckel, Kintel, and Dryrie joined the fray, and the dark elves were scattered among the woods. After each and every one of them had perished, the winged elves sailed up into the heavens, free to bask in the light of the stars and listen to their songs, to gaze at the celestial wonders and live forever in awe and the deepest of peace.

As the day ended, trudging along the snow with Santa in the lead were Myckel, Kintel, Dryrie, Faybin and a whole host of elves. When the elves reached a cabin in the woods, a small figure dressed in white stepped out. It was Santa’s betrothed, Linnea.

“Santa!” she exclaimed, racing for him.

He lifted her up and embraced her closely. Placing her back down, he gazed into her eyes and said meaningfully, “The King of the Elves can only marry an elven princess.”

Linnea’s face fell.

With his finger, he raised her countenance. A tear trailed down her cheek, but Santa surveyed her with a twinkle in his eye. He touched her ears and said,

"You have the most beautiful ears."

Her ears, the elves were amazed to see, had transformed and now ended in elegant pointed tips. And on her back was a pair of beautiful wings.

"Oh! Why bless us and save us! If I haven't seen everything, now! You've gone and sprouted wings, Linnea, my dear!" cried her aunt from the doorway.

Later, as the day ended, Santa, having visited his Tawdle parents who were most overjoyed to see him, sat gazing up at the stars with Myckel. Myckel asked Santa what he planned to do.

"I will be free to roam Euchaia once a year. I cannot think of a better way to spend it than to bring peace and good will to men. They are in great need of things such as these."

Epilogue

Thus it is that Santa, except for one night and day every year, lives in the remotest part of the heavens. While very remote, I cannot say that it is entirely lonely, for his elven friends visit him often and of course his wife is there, too. Where is it, you ask? I'll leave that for another story.

When he does come to Euchaia that one special time a year, I can't say that Santa has a gift for each and every girl and boy, woman or man, but I do know that with his elven ears he will hear the call of one who believes, no matter the distance, and such a sound, as you might imagine, brings his heart the greatest joy. The one who wishes to find that package labeled, "From Santa" will have a very difficult challenge on his hands. But his gifts are there just the same, perhaps under the tree, perhaps in a stocking, perhaps in the hands of a stranger at the mall or in a market and often delivered not by him, but by his unsuspecting agents: you and me.

Still, the greatest gift that he brings, he brings to everyone who wants it, both young and old, and that is Christmas spirit. For the hopeful eye that gazes up to the sky on that special night on the twenty-fourth of December will sometimes spot that small streak of light that marks his coming, and the ear that listens most carefully for his voice can no doubt hear the echo of his warm greeting, “Love one and all, give gifts and do right! A merry morning to all, and to all a good night!”

The End

Thank you for reading! Preseption Press and the author sincerely hope that you enjoyed this story. Your review on Amazon.com and Goodreads.com would be greatly appreciated.

To learn more about B.C.CHASE, and for free book offers, visit bcchase.com.

Visit the official B.C.CHASE page at www.facebook.com/paradeisia

For more elves, dragons, goblins, and magic, don't miss *Santa Claus: The King of the Elves*, the unabridged version.

SANTA CLAUS: THE KING OF THE ELVES

THE EPIC UNABRIDGED EDITION OF THE #1 BESTSELLING CHRISTMAS BOOK ON AMAZON.COM

When Santa's true love, Linnea, is kidnapped, he and his loyal High Elf friends embark on an enthralling journey across the perilous lands of Euchaia in a desperate bid to bring her safely home, little realizing that much more is at stake than

Linnea's life. By the end, the very survival of all High Elves is in jeopardy and Santa makes a fateful choice between his love for her and the destiny of the elves.

In this spellbinding adventure, internationally bestselling author B.C.CHASE taps the furthest reaches of his mesmerizing imagination to weave a suspenseful tale featuring seafaring dwarves, fiery dragons, cultured goblins, and flying elves that culminates in a battle of epic proportions.

Made in the USA
San Bernardino, CA
07 November 2017